CW00432939

Contents

Foreword

The phone rang and my wife went to answer it. I was in the front room and could hear her engaged in conversation. From her manner, it was clear that the caller was not a friend, relative or business contact - or even a wrong number. I was mildly intrigued but I carried on reading my book. Finishing the conversation, she entered the front room with a rather mystified air. "I've just been speaking to a lovely gentlemen who rang us thinking that we were publicists hoping that we could help him publish his work."

"Oh, I see what does he do?"
"He writes short stories and poetry."
"Right, ok."
"I said that maybe you would like to help him."

Of course, we aren't publicists but somehow we have been listed on the internet as such! Nevertheless, I was intrigued enough to meet the gentleman concerned - Rodney Pilkington.
Fortunately, he lived just down the road from where we do. So I turned up at his house not really knowing what to expect. I was greeted by a lovely, unassuming gentleman with a genuine manner and a modest bearing. We hit it off straight away. He invited me to read 'Penny From The Stars', and I was immediately smitten by his work.

His writing is characterised by a gentle, homely humour and abrupt startling twists. Often his themes mine the rich seam of a post-war Lancashire childhood, living in a small country hamlet many miles from civilisation. Kids had to make up their own entertainment and they often did so by going on various adventures. But that was all part of growing up. Anyone over a certain age who has had a normal upbringing with all its thrills and spills will be transported back to their own childhood by reading these captivating tales of boyish adventure.

But this collection boasts not only quaint tales of a Lancashire Mark Twain; Rod also casts a satirical eye at the vagaries of the workplace and the cronyism and partiality of society. No rancour is involved, however: just a raised eyebrow and the gentle twinkle of humour.

It is the story which is always the main thing for Rod - for within these deceptively simply stories he displays the art of the born story teller, often reserving the meaning and true intent of the story until the final sentence.

Readers often want to know something of the author, and within this collection Rod discloses something of himself. There are vignettes of ordinary life: parents seeing a young man off on a night out, families having heart to hearts or going through a typical holiday trauma. You see Rod at heart is a family man with a true reverence for family life, and these stories paint such pictures with lovely tenderness and fellowship.

Although not featured within this collection Rod is also a poet, and for anyone interested there is also a collection of his poems available (also called 'The Journey Back'). Rod is pretty much a self taught poet and his work betrays little influence from others. In fact, Rod admits that he rarely reads much poetry. That fact to me, does not subtract anything from his work: they are pithy poems, written in free verse with little embellishment. Their guiding principle often simply seems to be - say something well with few words. Some are sublimely romantic, others philosophical or even visionary, but there are many which are homely, and unashamedly sentimental even. Nevertheless, Rod cannot help but indulge his playful sense of humour, and it is this overriding aspect that - like the man himself - carries over and binds together this collection which is to treasure, and also to enjoy at leisure.

Michael Coupe July 2018

There are some people in life that make you laugh a little louder, smile a little bigger, and live just a little bit better.
- Unknown Author

I'd give all wealth that years have piled,
The slow result of Life's decay,
To be once more a little child
For one bright summer day.
~Lewis Carroll, "Solitude"

What we remember from childhood we remember forever —
permanent ghosts, stamped, inked, imprinted, eternally seen.
~Cynthia Ozick

TO VIKKI

KINDEST REGARDS
FROM ROD.

[signature]

5

SEPT 2018.

Penny From The Stars

Day 1

"A penny for them?"
'"What?"
"Your thoughts..."
"Oh, I was just looking in wonder at the stars."
"Alright sir, I'll leave you in peace, goodnight."
"Goodnight officer."

I suppose the copper was a little puzzled to see a young man sat alone on the sea front. Anyway, when he spoke to me I was in a sort of trance, I suppose. My thoughts had taken me back to my childhood. I was sitting at my desk taking a science lesson. Our teacher was a delightful eccentric and allowed us to listen to a recording of the radio series called *Journey Into Space*. He was called Mr Crabtree. In our next term for some reason our teacher changed which was very disappointing as we had to return to the curriculum.
By the way, my name is Ken Sivoh; I am 22 years old but I will be 23 on the 12th of August 1967. As I speak, the sound of my voice is being recorded on the new portable tape recorder which I hope to use as a diary. This fairly new technology interests me, but the real reason why I am using it is because I want to record my thoughts as a kind of diary. It is the 6th of July 1967 and I am enjoying the first day of a week-long holiday in Blackpool. I am not alone; I'm with my mum and dad. This might seem a bit strange but there is a reason (apart from the fact that I still live at home). I should have been on holiday with my friends - three young men call Easy, Shebe and Wilmer - in Benidorm. Unfortunately, and much to my embarrassment, I got cold feet and couldn't for the life of me board the plane at Manchester

Airport, even when that captain said I could sit with him.   So here I am with Mum and Dad - I feel a bit of a 'Mary Ann'!

Day 2

It is the 7th July, our landlady, Mrs Pucket, cooked a very nice breakfast for all her guests. During our meal, I noticed my mum and dad were about the youngest people in the digs - apart from myself. Anyway, I returned to my room - the main reason being the rain. However, the weather forecast says that it's going to stop during the afternoon, so until then I'm going to chill out on my bed and record a poem:

Down today, very low,
All my negative thoughts are in tow.
At this moment in time,
I can't imagine a steeper decline.
Although at the bottom of this abyss,
I'm still thinking of how to climb the cliff.
As I scan the recorded memories in my mind,
I try to review in small part,
Glimpses of happy moments that might lift my heart.

"Ken, Ken, Ken!"
"What?"
"Ken."
"Oh, it's you Mum."
"Ken, I couldn't wake you."
"Blimey Mum, what's the panic?"
"Oh, no panic love, it's just your dad and me are going out now and I was wondering if you wanted to come with us?'
"Where are you going?"
"We're just going to Stanley Park."

"No thanks Mum, I might have a walk on the prom this afternoon."

"It's afternoon now, you must have been asleep for about three hours."

"Oh, right you carry on, I'll do my own thing shortly.".

"Oh Ken, just before I go... I've been talking to Mrs Pucket and she mentioned that her daughter was living back at home and is at a bit of a loose end, so I said our Ken would take her out one evening."

"Blimey Mum!"

"Oh Ken, it won't hurt will it?"

"Ok, then when can I meet her?"

"She'll be home from work at tea time."

"Right ok Mum, oh Mum what's her name?"

"She's called Penny."

Day 3

"Morning Ken, love"

"Morning Mum."

"Ken, I couldn't talk at breakfast - I didn't want Mrs Pucket to hear me - I just wanted to ask you how you got on with Penny last night?"

"Oh it was fine, we went to the slot machines and then to a coffee shop. We had a good chin wag. She was saying that her job is as a nurse on the A&E ward at Blackpool Victoria Hospital. She seems to enjoy the work. However, working on the ward can be trying at times regarding accident victims etc."

"Did she mention her husband?"

"Yes, it seems that most of their problems stem from him being very possessive. This has resulted in the separation."

"Do you think that she could be the one?"

Blimey Mum, I only met the girl yesterday and she's married and just separated! But I must admit, she has been on my mind..."

"Ken, when I met your dad I was just the same, but your dad was quite different. When we had been going out for a few months I said to him 'Would you ever consider getting married?' And he said, 'Women are like elephants to me - I like looking at them but I wouldn't like to own one'."

"I can believe that Mum, he isn't the most romantic type is he?"

"That's right Ken, I think most policemen aren't."

"You might have something there mum 'cos that's what Penny's husband does for a living- he's called PC Lionel Black."

Day 4

"Ken, me and Dad are going on the tram to Fleetwood market. Have you any plans for today?"

"Yes Mum, I'm going out with Penny. Penny's shift changes today so we are going out during the afternoon."

"Ken love, I must say you look like a new man since you met Penny. I know it's only been a few days but you have bucked-up completely."

"Steady on, Mum, 'new man' blimey! I had been feeling a bit 'cat melodeon'. Last weekend, when I didn't go to Benidorm with the boys..."

"What's this 'cat melodeon'?"

"Oh, it's just a saying young people say when they are feeling crap."

"I'll try to remember that saying for when your dad's getting on my nerves. Ken, your friends Shebe, Easy and Wilmer are nice young men, but some of your other friends are not really suitable."

"You might be right Mum, but I haven't seen Bunger and Owerdy for years. They are due to be released from the young offender's

prison next year for causing that train trash. And my other childhood friends: Cute, Plodney, Kye and Lacker are due to be released this August for their part in connection with the 'Detonator Gang' - quite a motley crew eh, Mum?"
"Yes Ken, they are really not the type a policeman's son should be hanging around with!"
"Ok Mum, I will see you later, don't make Dad spend too much, ha-ha!"

Day 5

Thursday, I'm recording my diary; just had breakfast, another Full English! I must have put on a couple of pounds this week. Anyway, we are going for a walk when it stops raining. That is Mum, Dad, Penny and me. I have suggested we book for the *End of the Pier Show* this evening. However, Penny has to start work at six so won't be able to go. But I don't think she was too keen on seeing Roy Chubby Brown - his act is a little too close to the bone! The other top of the bill act is the pop band, *The Four Pennys*. They had a number one hit record called *Juliet* back in 1964. The lead singer, Lionel Morton was a choir boy at Blackburn Cathedral. I think it will be a good show.
Yesterday, I had a really good talk with Penny; she has been quite sanguine despite the problem with her marriage. She told me that their problems stem from the fact that she married Lional knowing that she was not in love with him. She felt that she couldn't break his heart by leaving him, but trying to live up to his expectations was getting progressively more difficult. Initially, it was flattering that an older man was in love with a girl ten years his junior but it has been the biggest mistake of her life. I replied that most people know when their feelings are correct: even at a very young age I knew the depth of feeling required for a relationship to be complete. But I suppose you can't blame some people for just wanting companionship even if

10

there are regrets at times - especially when one of them needs 24 hour care.

However, I must say that while Penny and I have only known each other for a short time our quiet times are bliss - minutes turn to hours and our unspoken thoughts seem to be mutually understood.

Day 6

Morning...

I have woken up this morning with a 'bee in my bonnet'. Prior to this holiday, I had felt settled in my life - working at the Midland Bank in Burnley, seeing my mates at Burnley Football Club and going out on regular Saturday nights at the Mecca Ballroom. Whilst knowing that meeting Penny had left a profound impression on me, I didn't ever imagine that my habits of a lifetime could suddenly seem so very much less important. However, my new happiness is also tinged with a new, inexplicable feeling of foreboding. I suppose it's only natural to worry exaggeratedly about something happening to a friend or family member - or indeed oneself.

"Oh Ken!"
"Yes Dad! What's happening?"
"Your mother and me are going out now. We thought we would get the tram to Star Gate and then have a walk on the sand hills."
"Ok Dad, I will see you later; I'm going with Penny to the Cash & Carry."
"Ok Son, see you later."

As usual the day has passed far too quickly and all too soon. Penny went off to work. I sat in the lounge and watched *Dr Kildare*. Mum and Dad had asked if I wanted to go with them to the Grand Theatre where Wilfred Pickles & Mabel were performing their show, *Have a Go Joe*. I wasn't in the mood for anything as frivolous as that. I was just thinking that it's mine and Penny's last night together and then I'm heading back to Burnley in the morning.

Later that same evening, as I relaxed on my bed listening to local radio I was stunned by a news bulletin. A news reader announced: "We just have had a report of a man being seriously injured by what is thought to have been a penny apparently thrown from the top of Blackpool Tower."
The report switched to an eyewitness: "I was on the pavement at the foot of the tower, and the policeman was just a few feet in front of me. He was standing with his back to the wall and seemed to be looking at the night sky." The reporter then asked about the penny: "I saw it bounce off his head and both of them hit the pavement. When the ambulance came, the paramedics lifted him onto a stretcher and as they put him into the ambulance I could see the imprint of King George V right in the centre of his forehead. He was taken to Blackpool Victoria Hospital."
A hospital spokesperson reported that the patient named as P.C. Lional Black was in a critical condition. The news report has left me in a daze. I thought about Penny and the shock she must have had when her husband was brought into A&E. After that I collected my thoughts and went to talk to Mrs Pucket. However, she had already been told about the accident - Penny had phoned her from the hospital.

When Mum and Dad returned from the theatre, they couldn't believe it! Good grief, it is no wonder, is it?

Day 7

It's Saturday morning; Mum and Dad have left for home and I have made plans to stay on another week. Mum and Dad are travelling by train so they arranged for a taxi to take them to the South shore Train Station. We said our goodbyes as the taxi pulled away. Next, Mrs Pucket walked in to the lounge where I was sitting.
"Ken." she said.
"Yes, Mrs Pucket."
She told me that Penny's husband had passed away during the night.
Meanwhile, Mum and Dad arrived at the station. "Mabel, we have a few minutes before the train leaves; I'll just pop to the kiosk for a morning paper and a packet of spangles."
"Ok, Albert."
"Keep your eye on the cases."
My dad went to the kiosk to get a paper and returned pale and trembling.
"Albert, what is it you look like you've seen a..."
"Mabel! Mabel! There's been a terrible plane crash!"
"Where?"
"In Manchester, a plane arriving from Benidorm - engine failure - all on board killed!"
"Oh, my God!"

Four For Whittle Pike Quarry

Ah! The marvel of technology that was our first television set. It's 1956 and my mum and dad have spent a small fortune on our *Bush* television set: £60 in fact! Just in time for the Olympic games in Australia, I thought! There would be no Satellite link to beam live pictures to us, of course. We would have to watch a version recorded a number of days earlier. These were screened during the day when Mum and Dad were at work. So my mate Pod and I watched great athlete's such as Gordon Perry, the middle distance runner and many others, who gave us such excitement the like of which we had never felt before!

By the way, my name is Shebe and I was 11 years old at the time this occurred. My home was a small hamlet called Strongstry which is made up of mill workers cottages which and been built about 1845 by the local mill owner. Both Mum and Dad worked at the mill. Our homes are fairly isolated with just the one small shop in our village. Also, it is a fair walk to the nearest main road.

Pod and I were mainly interested in sport: cricket in the summer and football in winter. Back then, it was July so we played cricket almost every day. Pod was 10 years old and lived a couple of doors down from me. His dad worked at the mill also. His mum was a stay-at-home mum due to having five children at home.

Most of the kids in our homes were born in the years just after the Second World War. I was born in 1945 and Pod in 1946, and as both of our fathers were young enough, they served in the armed forces: Pod's in the Territorial Army and mine in the Royal Air force. Dad was part of the Ground Crew. His job was to refuel the aircraft. The war was tough on both the men and the women. While the men went to war, the woman left behind had to take up the slack. Both Pod's mum and mine had been important loom weavers during the war.

As I said, most kids in Strongstry were around my age. However, about five kids had been born during the early years of the 1940s, mainly to older parents and were therefore a little older. Two such boys were both 15 and nicknamed Panda and Chess. Panda was a big lad for his age, known more for his engineering ability than his sensitivity. One didn't find him usually on the cricket or football field. More often than not, he could be found tooling away in a garage or his bedroom working on motorbikes or model aircraft. Regarding his nickname, it was to do with his ears, they stuck out like airplane wings - and he *was* actually sensitive to them, so it wasn't wise to mention his nickname to his face. Pod and I looked up to him though, and we eagerly anticipated his next model airplane's first flight. The other boy, Chess, was similar in regard to his lack interest in sport. His nickname was quite apt as he was unpredictable at times. Just a few weeks ago he came to join a group of us holding a bow and arrow. Without warning, he fired an arrow straight up into the air and we all looked up in the air, holding our hands above our heads. I was unlucky and the arrow came down and went through the webbing between my thumb and forefinger. Chess had fixed a darning needle into the arrow head. Despite this kind of behaviour Pod and I liked him, also. Whenever we saw Panda and Chess we would always approach them hoping that they would include us.

And lo and behold, the chance came on a sunny day on the 14th July. Pod and I were sitting on a low wall which surrounded the gable end of the village shop. Panda and Chess strolled past pretending not to notice us. However, we ran up to them asking what they were up to. They said that they were going up to the quarry on Whittle Pike. Pod and I were well aware of this quarry as it could be seen from an area called The Plunge. The

15

Plunge was what we used to call a stream which sourced high up on the moors. During the summer months kids would paddle and picnic on the its banks. High above The Plunge, one could see a tall concrete chimney projecting from the quarry. It was used to remove exhaust fumes generated by the machines used around the mine and quarry areas.   "Can we come with you, Chess?" I cried.
"I'm not sure, lads, it could be dangerous."
"Please, we'll be careful!" pleaded Pod.
"Ok, come on then!"

Heading out of Strongstry, our path moved to the east by the side of the river Irwell, walking against the flow. Before long, we crossed the fairly new concrete and steel bridge that the mill owners had built to enable the workers' children to attend Stubbins school. This stood on the steep hill north of Stubbins, and within the boundaries of the hamlet of Chatterton. Working our way through this small hamlet, we saw on our left rows of small cottages built for mill workers around 1800 (much older than the houses we lived in). Opposite these was Chatterton Park on which Aichens Mill had once stood. This land is famous for being the location of the Chatterton Riots. In 1826 rioters from Blackburn, Haslingden and other local towns had smashed the power looms in many mills during a two or three day wrecking spree. The rioters had blamed the machines for taking their jobs. The government in response had alerted the army who were ready and waiting when 3,000 rioters arrived at Aichens. Six rioters were killed and many injured. However by the 1930s, the land had become a park and a playground.

"Chess, why are you not carrying your gun today?" I said
"No slugs and it's not wise to have it with me when we get to the main road: don't want the Bobbies to see it."

As I looked across the park, it reminded me of a football match from last season, played against the Chatterton lads. In most matches we came off worse; but in our defence we were always going to be up against it for the Chatterton lads were three or four years older. One lad, Jingles, must have been about 18 years old, but for all that he was no world beater; in fact could have been one of the first people in the world to have played Walking Football. He only seemed to take a passing interest, playing with one hand in his pocket and jingling his loose change.

Just after the park, on the left stood a detached house which would have belonged to the mill owner. Across the road on the right, is St Phillip's Church. The church, together with its Sunday school was built in 1936. Pod and I had attended both and presently we were in fact choir boys. Then we turned a sharp left and started to climb up Chatterton Lane. At the top of the lane, we bore left onto the main road which took us to Edenfield Village. On entering the village, we took a sharp right onto Bury Road. After about 200 yards we made a sharp left onto a narrow track which would eventually take us to the moors. As we made our way along, in the near distance a small semi-derelict cottage came into view.

"I can't ever remember seeing that place before, can you Pod?" said I.
"Yes, I've seen it once, you must have come to The Plunge the other way from Gin Croft Lane."
"Oh, I see".

As we got closer, I could see an old man sat by the door smoking his pipe. "Where are you for, lads?" he said.
No one spoke.
"Has the cat got your tongue?"

Pod decided to tell him. "We're going up to the quarry."
"If thee are, tha mern't go int' Royal Mine. Thad roof is in a
state."
Chess and Panda ignored the old man but Pod was intrigued:
"Oh, is it?"
"Take no notice of him, what does he know about mines. If we
don't go inside the Drift Mine, how are we going to find any tools
left by miners when the quarry closed?" said Panda.
I asked Chess whether he was up to going into the mine.
"Not sure until I check it out."

Shortly after, we came to The Plunge picnic area. The stream
was a gentle, lazy flow in this area due to the land levelling out.
We crossed the stream and started on the gentle grass slopes.
High up in the distance we could see the plateau on which the
Whittle Pike Quarry stood.
"The quarry hasn't been worked since the 1920s." said Panda.
"Why not?" asked Pod.
"The usable stone had been exhausted by then. Also, the
building boom due to the industrial revolution had eased."

After about 20 minutes climbing, the grass thinned out; the
slope became dominated by heather and cotton buds. In front of
us appeared a steep man-made bank of semi-loose screed and
broken rock chippings. Further to the right, I could see the slope
wasn't as steep and actually more grassy. Pod had seen it, too.

"Can we go that way?" he asked.
"No," replied Panda, "This is the only way up."
I pointed to the top of the screed: "What would happen to us if
we fall from up there?"
"You would be killed," said Panda.

Silence fell amongst us like sudden blow. I was starting to wish
that I hadn't come along.   But it was too late - I couldn't afford
to lose face by turning tail and running for it like a frightened
rabbit. Plus, I still wanted to see the quarry.   I looked at Pod; I
could see that he was thinking the same. So we all carried on as
before, but now I could feel the icy knot of fear gripping my
insides

As we started to climb, it didn't seem as bad as I first thought.
Panda had gone on ahead on his own but at least Chess was
behind me, so I felt a little safer.   Pod was some way ahead of
me. Without warning there was a shout, "Help!"
I looked up and saw Pod slowly sliding down the face of the
screed. He had only been about six feet from the summit. Panda
appeared suddenly and shouted, "Don't be a pansy, grab the
bigger rocks!"
Pod had started panicking though and was frozen in a crab-like
position. He started to cry out loud. When Panda saw that Pod
was beyond helping himself, he relented and climbed down
behind him and pushed him up from behind.   Once at the top,
Pod was still a bit upset but he soon got over it.   I said, "Can we
go down the easier way when we're going home?"
"Ok," said Chess.

We had finally arrived at the quarry. It was blooming
marvellous. The top of the hill had been quarried away to leave
a plateau. At the rear, about 50 yards away was the entrance to
the coal mine. It was a drift mine, which means basically that it
was dug almost horizontally into the side of the hill. It ran
across the moorland and we could see the track of it as it
crossed the moor. It was obvious that the roof had collapsed in
several places - small pits dotted the surface of the ground here
and there.

As we started to nose around the quarry, we were delighted to see that all the steam powered cranes were still there and had been left almost completely intact. Pod and I couldn't resist but to climb up into the seats of these massive great machines and pretend to operate them. Panda and Chess meanwhile, were busy looking for discarded tools. At one point, Panda climbed down a big hole in the quarry and seemed to be gone for quite a while. As we looked on anxiously, he suddenly emerged with a big smile and with a lump hammer in tow!

Then the instruction came from Panda: the one Pod and I were dreading, " Come on lads, let's have a look into the mine!" Panda led the way, followed by Chess and then Pod and I (not exactly holding hands but not far off!) The walls of the coal mine were about six feet broad and the roof was about the same height. In retrospect, nobody in their right mind would have walked into this deadly, disused mine. However, we did! As we walked, we could see the black coal seam running horizontally along the walls in thin lines. After a few minutes, l looked back and saw that the entrance had reduced to a small circle of light in the distance. I nudged Pod to show him. Pod and I then asked almost simultaneously, "How much further are we going on?"

"Not much further," Chess replied, "We'll go to the first roof fall. As long as we can still see we'll be alright. Keep your eyes open for any tools. "
"I can hardly see, let's go back," said Pod.
"Just hang on a minute," ordered Panda, "I can see a pickaxe handle sticking out of this rubble."

Panda started trying to pull it free. He was banging the larger pieces of rubble with his lump hammer. Even Chess started to get jumpy: "Don't do too much banging it's too..." Just as he spoke the roof behind us almost silently collapsed with a slow whoosh followed by a soft thud. Dead silence followed and complete blackness.

 Eventually Panda spoke up, "Are you ok lads?"

More silence.

Then Pod and I shook off our shock and shouted in unison:

"We're trapped! We're trapped what shall we do?"

Panda tried to calm us all down, "I've got this pickaxe out, don't worry lads, I'll hack our way out of it in no time."

"Yes, but what if a bit more roof comes down with all the banging?" said Chess.

"Right ok, I hadn't thought of that," admitted Panda, "I'll try to scrape a narrow gap through the rubble."

By this time, Pod and I were in tears; the roof had caved in behind us trapping us in. Added to that, we had no idea how *much* had fallen and consequently how much there was to tunnel through. All that could be said was that at least we were all still together and that none of us were hurt. I started to chatter, stating the obvious about how we're trapped in the dark with no water and no food and I was quite lost in my soliloquy of despair when I heard a sudden crunch.

"Pod, is that you eating something?"

"Yes, how do you know?"

"I can hear you crunching!"

"It's only a pig nut; I dug up a couple with my pen knife on the way up. Do you want one?"

"Yes it's better than nowt!"

"Think yourself lucky Shebe!" said Pod.

As the hours ticked by, we all began to fear the worst. "I think we've had it." said Chess, "That pickaxe is never gonna be enough to shift that lot, and no one knows where we are. My mum and dad will be home from work at 5:30, Pod's dad about

21

six, but with absolutely no idea where to look for us. All of us were now thinking that this could be our last day on earth.

Panda had given up trying to dig us out. We all squatted down with our backs to the wall of the tunnel. We had no idea what time it was. Chess had a watch but he couldn't see it in the dark. By now, even the big lads were sobbing silently. As I sank deeper in despair I said a silent prayer. As I did I heard a voice in my head. It was the first time I ever heard this sound and it has never happened again in my life. It came low and clear and had a lovely dulcet tone. "I love you" were the only words spoken but it immediately raised my spirits. I stood up and declared that I thought that everything was going to be alright. Still nothing happened straightaway. Then, after what seemed like forever:

"Shermon! Shermon! Can you hear me?"
"Dad! Dad! Yes I can!" I cried, "How did you know I was here?"
"Oh, never mind that now I'm with an old miner who used to work this mine, he's going to get you out!"

Sure enough, within a short time and after a bit of judicious digging and the use of some timber props, an opening appeared before us. Two faces appeared in the light - Dad and the old miner we had seen further down the hill. "Dad, how did you know where to find us?"
"Well, when you and Pod weren't home by seven, Pod's dad and I decided to look for you. Pod's dad went west, to the area known as Buckden and I went east, to Chatterton. As I walked though Chatterton, I bumped into our vicar, Reverend Day. He said had seen two of his choir boys going up Chatterton Lane around 12 noon. Then I worked out where you might be heading. I think you might recognise Mr Whittaker, the man who warned you not to enter the mine?"

22

On the way home, Chess and Panda were quiet; they just tagged along behind us.

"Dad."

"Yes, Shermon"

"Do you think that Pod might get a good hiding off his dad?"

"No, I think he will get away with just a telling off. His dad told me that Pod's grandma had won the Irish Sweep Stake and had given his dad £20."

"Pod, did you hear that?"

"Yeah I did, yahooooo!"

That evening, as I relaxed in my bed my thoughts drifted back and forth: first, to the wonders of television and the marvel of being able to watch the Olympic Games in my front room; second, to the almost ancient machinery used to excavate the local quarry all those years ago; and thirdly on the power of love, which can't be dug up, removed and hoarded or ever mechanically engineered.

Wanted – Volunteer to be shot

Bunger was bent over, chopping wood. This was his part of the arrangement. Bunger had only had his name for about a year. Prior to that, his name was Clog due to his footwear. Bunger was a sturdy lad for his twelve years. He was a surly type who didn't smile much and hardly ever laughed, but he was a worker and would have plenty of firewood ready for when his pals returned.

Just then a voice behind him said: "I've only got a bucket half-full Bunger!"

"Lazy get Owerdy!"

"Well, if you want any more you can go and git it Bunger!"

Bunger didn't say anything, he just kept working. Owerdy was a small, thin, nine year old boy with a head of white hair. An introverted boy with a nasty streak, he was kept in check however, by his older friends. He was the youngest member of the group. Owerdy's job had been to collect coal. To do this he had to climb the wall to get on to the railway line and pick up small pieces of coal that had fallen from the steam trains as they rounded the bend. This was a dangerous job as he wouldn't be able to hear an oncoming train until it was right on him. Also, he had to look out for the railway workmen. These were the platelayers who maintained the track. If he was caught he would get a thick ear.

"They're taking their time, aren't they?" said Owerdy.

 It found deaf ears, so Owerdy sat on the grass just to the side of where Bunger was starting to light a small fire. He was using the flat concrete base of the recently demolished institute. This building had been set in an area called 'The Pen' - for years earlier it had been used to pen chickens. The institute had been built with its back to the mainline - one of two railway lines

24

which straddled the remote, small hamlet where the boys lived. Although the two lines ran past the hamlet they didn't stop there. In fact, the hamlet was so isolated that there wasn't even a main road within two miles, just a narrow, private road linking it to the outside world.

Just then Owerdy spotted two figures climbing the small hill towards the small plateau where the fire was roaring.

"Come on Kye!"
Kye ignored him, so he tried again,
"Come on Sivoh!"
Sivoh shouted back in a muffled tone, "Ok, keep your shirt on!"

Sivoh's real surname was Brown so he got his name from the brand of brown bread - 'Hovis' - spelled backwards. He was a slightly tubby boy of 13 who happened to be extremely bright. He was an only child whom the other boys thought spoilt. And in some ways he was, but this was only in a very comparative sense, for none of the boys lived in the lap of luxury.

Kye, on the other hand, was a well built 12 year old, quite old-fashioned in many ways, but enjoyed any form of work as long as he didn't get his shoes dirty - they had to stay clean at all cost! He contrived this by standing on one leg and rubbing the top front of his boots with the back of his knee-length stockings.

Kye and Sivoh arrived two minutes later.

"How have you gone on?" Bunger asked
"All right," replied Sivoh.
"Two large potatoes and a block of lard," said Kye.

They had been to the only shop in the hamlet and bought these by mustering together a few pennies.

"Peel the spuds Owerdy!" Bunger ordered.

But Owerdy had already begun to do just that using his penknife with quick, incisive movements. Bunger was just as swift, melting the lard in an old can over the fire. Twenty minutes later the boys were eating chips.

Bunger kept the fire going after their meal. It was the height of summer with good warm weather, but the boys still enjoyed a good fire. Earlier, in the morning, they had been playing cricket and were ready for a rest. Just then, two figures appeared at the top of the hill. The boys watched them but didn't speak. The two figures arrived at the little camp. One of the two spoke to the boys.

"Are we late?"
"Yeah," said Bunger, "Nowt left."

This one was an older boy called Chess. He was 15 years old, quite tall with a shock of fair hair. Although he also lived in the hamlet he was rarely seen, at least by the younger boys. His companion was a much younger boy called Easy. Easy was 12 years old and of average height. He was a gentle soul who enjoyed model railways and nature. He was also a fantastic climber, hence his name.
Earlier that day, Chess had called on Easy (who had been working on a model railway station) and the two boys then decided to get some fresh air. Chess was a very affable boy whom the others looked up to, despite him being a bit unpredictable. He wasn't into sport but had a bike -as had Easy - which set them apart from the others whose parents couldn't afford these things.
The other thing to note is that Chess always carried a gun with him - an air rifle, in fact.
Kye spoke first, "Chess, can I have a go with the rifle?"
"Ok Kye, but only one shot, I've not got many slugs."

26

Kye took the gun and aimed for an old tin can about ten yards way. He missed. The boys all laughed, even Bunger. Chess said, "It's not all your fault Kye, this gun is pretty well worn out, there's not much strength in the spring anymore. It's so weak it wouldn't hurt if you were shot with it."

Easy laughed, "I wouldn't want to be shot by that whatever condition it is in!"

Chess continued, "Here Kye, get hold of it. When I tell you, shoot me in the back."

Chess moved about ten feet, turned his back on Kye then shouted,

"Fire!"

"Are you sure?"

"Yeah, do it."

Kye fired and everyone could see the pellet strike Chess in the back. He made not a sound. Then he turned around casually and sauntered back to the group.

"Didn't hurt at all."

Everyone was flabbergasted and fell silent.

"Does anyone else want to volunteer to be shot?" Chess asked:

"What about you Bunger?"

"No way!"

"Sivoh, what about it?"

"You must be joking."

"I'll do it," said Owerdy.

"No" said Chess, "You're too young and scrawny."

"I'm not!"

"Yes you are," said Kye, "I'll do it."

"Ok," said Chess, "Tell me when you're ready."

"Just a minute..." Kye started to clean his boots using the back of his stockings.

"Come on, Kye!"

"Ok, Shoot!"

27

The gun went off...

"F***ing hell!" Were the only words that came from Kye. When he turned round his face was ashen.

"Did it hurt, Kye?" asked Owerdy.

Kye was obviously in pain but he tried to put a brave face on.

Chess said, "I told you it wouldn't hurt."

But there were no more volunteers.

Shortly afterwards, most of the boys decided it was time to head home. Only Bunger and Owerdy were left sitting around the dying embers of the fire.

"Are you going home, Owerdy?"

"No not yet. My dad won't be home until about six."

"Mine won't either."

"Hey, Bunger, wasn't Kye a dick to let Chess shoot him?"

"You said, 'I'll volunteer'."

"I know, I know, but I would have changed my mind if he'd agreed."

"I think Kye was brave in a way. Chess was pretending it didn't hurt when he was shot."

"Yeah" said Owerdy, "He's a bit sly - he had a thick jacket on and Kye only had a shirt."

"Hey, Bunger, I've got a halfpenny!"

"Well? Big deal, one 'spanish' from t'shop, that's all that will buy."

"Yeah, I know. But one of the lads said if you lay a halfpenny onto a railway line it will be squashed until it looks like a well worn penny."

"Sounds ok, "said Bunger, "What time's the next train?"

"It's due about six o'clock."

"Right, let's do it."

28

They both climbed over the wall and onto the railway embankment.

"Have you got a watch Bunger?"

"No, have you?"

"You must be joking. I wish I had one, full stop."

"It must be nearly six."

He placed the coin onto the line, while Owerdy placed some of the white ballast stones onto the rail just a little further along.

"What are you doing?"

"I'm just putting these on t'line, we can watch it run over them."

The two boys climbed back over the wall and waited for the train.

Meanwhile, all the other boys had arrived home. Sivoh sat listening to the radio waiting impatiently for his tea. His mother said, "Tea won't be long, just waiting for your dad."

"Right, Mum, bit late isn't' he?"

Just then his dad walked in, seeming a little flustered.

"Mabel, there's been a terrible train crash!"

Robin Hood's Well

This story is of a time that no longer exists, a time when it was possible for young child to roam the English countryside in complete safety. At least from the threat of human beings. Care had only to be taken if climbing trees or crossing streams. Farm animals also, occasionally needed watching out for - especially when crossing a field of young bulls.

The main character in this story is a small boy called Pod. The name is a shortening of his Christian name of Podreig. A name for which he had to thank his great, great grandfather, Poadeereig Mcdermott who had arrived in England from Ireland in 1848.   At this time, many families had emigrated to England or America, Canada, Australia and a few other countries in order to escape from poverty and famine. Pod was an eight years old in 1950. His home was a small hamlet which comprised thirty-five terraced houses and one grocer.

These had been built a hundred years ago by the local land owner who owned a large textile mill. At its inception, it produced only woollen blankets, but now it also manufactured felt for the paper industry. Pod's father worked at this mill as did all the other men - and some women - who lived in the hamlet. Pod's father, like most young men, had served in the British armed forces during the war. He had been called up in 1940 and then trained at Fullwood barracks in Preston, before gaining his first posting at Liverpool. Their job was to guard the dock warehouses. At this time, the Liverpool docks were being heavily bombed.

"Dad said it was a terrifying experience," Pod used to recall.

His dad's next posting was to the south coast of England to prepare for a possible invasion after the fall of France. When this, fortunately, never materialized his father's battalion embarked from Portsmouth to Egypt. As they climbed the gangplank a dock worker was heard to say - "They won't see Blighty for at least three years."

That prophecy was to become fact. His wife was three months pregnant at the time and Pod was three and three months old when he met his father on his first home leave. And after another posting to India he finally arrived home in the summer of 1946 and was back to work at the mill within two weeks.

Some of the stories that Pod's father told him about his war exploits were amusing - like the time he stole one of the Ghurkha's knives. This was a feat not for the faint hearted: the Ghurkhas treated their knives almost like religious artefacts and this particular Ghurkha chased Pod's father as if his life depended on it! He also related how his friend who was killed by a Japanese booby trap. And about the bayonet wound in his side. Or else of the thoughts that went through a person's mind when they were hungry and thirsty - so hungry that they would eat anything and how he hoped Pod would never have to be in that situation.

However, Pod hadn't thought too deeply about the stories of the war. He wasn't alone in having a dad who had been in the army. All or most of his friends' fathers had also been soldiers. Of his few close friends only Cute - a boy living next door and whose father was a railwayman, didn't go to war. Cute's dad worked mainly on steam trains which hauled coal down the local branch line, coming from the coal mines of the Rossendale Valley and travelling ten miles to the town of Bury. Some days, as the train passed our hamlet, his dad would throw a large lump of coal down the embankment. He would pick it up on his way home in order to keep his home-fire burning. Cute, a boy with bushy, light brown hair and a slim build was quite tall for his age and was always hungry. If anyone was lucky enough to have an apple, Cute would always ask for the core.

Anyway, this summer morning Cute called for Pod. When I say 'call' I mean CALL! - for at this time, in most places in Lancashire, kids would stand near the back door and call out the Christian name of the particular child that you wanted to come out to play. If there were more than one or two calling it would end up becoming almost like a chorus!

Pod came to the door and the two of them then went to call for Shebe. Shebe was the same age as the other two boys, only much smaller and distinguished by gorgeous blond, curly hair. However, he wasn't backward at coming forward. He was quite capable of using any tactic when he was called upon to fight. Pod had found out this to his cost the last time they had had a disagreement - Shebe had sunk his teeth deep into his arm! Hopefully, there wouldn't be any of that sort of unpleasantness today. After Shebe there was just one more call remaining - for Panda. Normally, the pals couldn't really remember how nicknames arose but not in Panda's case - it was his ears. Panda's ears stood out like Prince Charles's did before he had the operation to pin them back. However, due to the fact that Panda was a big lad and 12 years old, it wasn't wise to mention his nickname to his face - only an exceptionally brave boy would risk that!

Panda was the guide for today's expedition, which as it happened, was to find and drink water from the well high on the moors where, according to legend, the most famous outlaw in the world had slaked his thirst - none other than Robin Hood.

32

He came to the door displaying his characteristic eccentricity. His interests lay not in football or cricket, preferring instead to tinker with mechanical things or build small model aircraft. Today for some reason, he arrived brandishing a viciously long spear.

The expedition took place during the school holidays when children look forward to six weeks break. The day was sunny and balmy. As the boys prepared to set off, the sound of singing broke the silence of the morning. 'Noise' was probably a more accurate description, however. The source was a teenage boy called Keith who had Down's Syndrome. The house where Keith lived had once been an old farmhouse which stood on the edge of the hamlet. It had been built 200 years previously. They would have to pass this place in order to follow a path running beside a stream which wound down from a place high on the moors - a three or four mile steep climb up from the hamlet. If Keith saw the group he would want to join in. However, despite Keith being a lovely, happy boy, this is something his mother would not allow, since the boys in the group were too young to be able to control a wilful 16 year old.

'Swish!' - Panda raked his spear around the boys heads making them duck down. And then sneaking past using a hedge for cover, he led the group still swishing his spear around their ears, forcing them to stay low to the ground for fear of losing an eyeball or two. As they passed a gap in the hedge, they could see Keith sitting on his swing which hung from a branch on the large weeping willow standing in the centre of a lawn. There was no fear that Keith would hear them as he sought to entertain everyone across a two mile radius with his take on 'singing'.

Once past Keith's house, the boys walked past the barn and followed a path which had been cut into the side of a deep gorge.

As Pod looked over a small stone wall to see the stream running passed, he recalled an adventure from the last Easter holidays. Panda, Shebe and Cute, listened as Pod recited the story of a climb he had undertaken along with two other pals called 'Easy' and 'Chess'.

"We were climbing down to the stream and had reached a very shaley rock section which we had to cross, when there was a shout from this wall at the top of the gorge. It was Easy's mother; she had arrived home from work in order to cook a meal for herself and Easy, and had somehow known where he would be. Anyway, she wasn't pleased at all to find him halfway down a 150 foot drop!"
Panda chimed in, "Why do some mothers always want to wrap their kids in cotton wool?"

When they had been walking for half an hour or so Cute decided to look for some 'pig nuts'. These were small round bulbs with the taste and texture of swede. To find them in the ground, he used to look for a spindly grass-like stalk with small delicate white flowers on top. Once he'd spotted one, he would then use a penknife to dig under the stalk and find the nut about an inch or so further down. It wasn't much of a snack but it filled a gap.

Swish! Out of nowhere Panda swung his spear just missing Shebe. "Hey, that only just missed," said Shebe.
"Think yourself lucky," replied Panda, "I wasn't aiming for you!"
Panda picked up his spear and strode off.

Meanwhile, Pod hadn't finished eating. He looked for a pink clover flower head. If one pulls these frail, thin stalks from the head, the small, white base has a sugary taste. As Pod enjoyed the sweet taste of the clover, his mind drifted back to the picnics he had been on at Buckden, where the local stream's torrent

slowed to form a lovely tranquil pond. At that point, a stone-built bridge crossed the stream.   This was used as a jumping-off point into the pool. However, as the water was very cold people would usually do no more than paddle.
"Right, come on!" said Panda, "Or we're never gonna get there."

Cute, however, was still down on his knees by the stream washing his hands after digging for pig nuts. Afterwards, he cupped them for a drink - much to Panda's disgust. He hadn't spoken a word since they left home. This was why his nick name was 'Cute' - he always had a dumb, innocent look on his face

By now they were leaving the wooded area.   As they approached the moorland, the lush grass disappeared to be replaced by heather. Shortly afterwards, they finished climbing and the land levelled out. A 'foreign free' silence suddenly prevailed: all noise from birds, the wind, and the boys idle chatter petered away to be replaced by the immanent splendour of the surrounding countryside. Habitation was just insignificant dark shapes far below.

Time passed, Shebe eventually seemed to get a little impatient and finally broke the powerful spell that bound them by using that well-worn child's refrain: "How far is it now?"
Panda replied "We're here."
"What?" said Pod, "We're here? Is that it?"

Pod, Shebe and Cute all looked down at a few rocks sticking out of the peaty ground where a small trickle of water appeared.

"Blimey!" said Shebe, "All that way just for this!"

Milestone

It's the evening of the 29th January 2013. I could say that it's a dark and stormy night, or it's a wind-swept snowy night. However, it's one of those nights which have become rare these days - it's a *foggy night*. Fog was something that we had plenty of years ago. In fact, I would say right up until the 1970s.

However, tonight it's a foggy night; not the kind of thick fog we used to call 'peasoupers', just wispy stuff, usually found over rivers or a reservoir. I think we all know that many things can jog one's memory (I find my main mood-changers to be weather, music or films) but this evening for some reason it is the fog that has put me in a reflective frame of mind. Deep in thought, I drift from melancholy bordering on mild depression to a more positive emotional state. However, being in a reflective mood, I realise that while I am basically a happy person, there are areas of my life that remain unfulfilled. These, which even extend to what I would call minor complications, can affect that balance of a person's life. It could be the arrival of a certain milestone without a satisfactory conclusion.

I recently watched a TV programme in which people were interviewed who had objected to the planning decision given to a building company's proposal for a new housing estate. It was obvious to the planners - and for that matter many neutral observers - that their plans were unobtrusive to nearby residents, but nevertheless the objectors still wanted to pursue their point of view. One old lady in particular, said the building would restrict the natural light into her lounge. The old lady's daughter and son-in-law also spoke on her behalf and argued strongly against the planning application. Other interviewees objected, also. When one or two people took the reins of the debate, others seemed to get an emotion lift from the camaraderie. Some were able to show emotions which probably had been latent for years. Regarding the old lady, I felt that the main reason for her opinion was the attention she was receiving from her family. People who are starved of affection will subconsciously take any route to receive it.

We all know there are many triggers which can affect one's psyche; and most people will agree that memories can be very emotionally provocative. Pondering this, I recalled childhood images recorded during the Easter holidays, some 59 years ago. Easter was early that year and it was still quite cold, but nevertheless undeterred, my friends and I decided to camp out overnight.

Leaving Strongstry early in the morning (a small hamlet where we lived) our plan was to camp in an area called 'Buckden': this was a strip of land which had been donated to the National Trust some years ago by the local landowning family. The land has a gentle slope up from Strongstry to the moorland about three miles away. The main feature of Buckden was the stream which had a source up on the moor before meandering down and entering the River Irwell at Strongstry.

It was still March, quite early in the year for camping out. A cool, light breeze blew but the day was clear and bright. Although we were only spending one night outside we weren't fully prepared for what we were about to experience.

Oh, and by the way my name is Dobbin - yes, I know quite a strange nickname. I earned it due to my size and strength and also being very tall. At five feet two inches and only eleven years old I tower above my pals. This is the reason I had the job of carrying our tent. It was pointed at the top - boy scouts use them - and it had been loaned to us by the vicar's son.

My companions were all boys - Wilmer, De Silento and Shebe. Wilmer, a lad of average build with dark hair had a kind disposition. However, he always carried a bow and arrow set and would fire in sharp order at any mice or rats he spotted. De Silento was very thin; he was nine years old but quite tall for his age. With white hair and bright blue eyes he was quite distinctive, and, as his name implies, he was very quiet. Finally, there was Shebe. Twelve years old, fairly small with blond curly hair, he was the brains of the group. However, his knowledge didn't cover camping or any of the practical jobs which had to be done!

After a two-mile trek, we found a piece of grass land quite close to the stream. Once we put the tent up, we started a fire and all sat round it chatting. After a few minutes, we decided to go on an expedition up on the moors, to try to reach the Pilgrim's Cross. It had originally been a large wooden cross when it had been first erected in the 13th century. And when the wood perished it was replaced by a stone-built obelisk several feet high. We had been informed that this could be found approximately two miles from the edge of the moor, slightly to the left.

Before moving on though we had a bite to eat. Our meal comprised 'jam butts' brought from home. 'Jam butts' are slices of bread and butter with fruit jam spread over. Some of the boys had this food every day, along with the other staple foods like 'chips'. Chips are sliced potato fried in lard. Many families lived on these two staples, mine included. Now, I am six foot two and 200 pounds, and my four brothers are bigger than me. Other boys who ate this diet also grew to at least six feet tall and became very athletic. Also, one needs to remember this was just

38

after the Second World War. The country had to ration food and most other commodities.

After four or five butties and a drink from the stream we started out on our expedition. Hoping that something exciting would happen and dressed only in shorts, a cotton shirt, jumper and pumps we set off. Our journey gently inclined for about one mile, in the course of which we reached a busy highway which had to be crossed since there was no way around. This road, adapted from an old cart track was dug approximately 150 years ago, but had recently been resurfaced to allow modern traffic from the north to travel to Bolton and then on to Manchester. Living in an old hamlet with little or no traffic meant that the very thought of crossing such a road filled us with some trepidation.

However the crossing passed without incident and we continued up a grassy gully until the Second World Ward 'Pill Box' came into view along with the large concrete blocks, which in the event of enemy invasion would have been used to block the road. The slight incline now became more like a fairly tough climb which continued until we reached what had been the original highway hundreds of years ago - just a cart track, really.

Once across, the land became as flat as a pancake. The moorland was spread out before us as far as the eye could see. Not having a compass or map to guide us, we were reliant solely on the directions we had been given.

"Come On!" shouted Wilmer impatiently at De Silento - who until now hadn't spoken a word.

In contrast, Shebe had been lecturing us all afternoon on the advantages of owning a slide rule. Wilmer also, was making a nuisance of himself by firing arrows at anything that moved. I was beginning to wonder where the Pilgrim's Cross was as we had been walking for what seemed a good half-hour. Even though none of us had a watch, we were able to live as animals do, taking note of the height of the sun. I suppose, if the day had been cloudy we would have had to guess the time. A short time later, we spotted it in the distance. Anything that stood above the heather could be seen quite easily against the skyline for the land was so flat. As we closed in, the monument could be seen more clearly, the original holy wooden cross had been replaced by a rather small, ugly grey block of stone with an inscription on it that read:

On this site stood the ancient Pilgrim's Cross. It existed in A.D. 1178 and probably reached back much earlier. Pilgrims to Whalley Abbey prayed and rested here

"We've made it, yippee!" shouted Wilmer trying to inject a bit of triumphalism into the muted atmosphere. We frowned in a puzzled way at it and maybe said a prayer or two, but no holy lights came from the sky. A few minutes later De Silento joined us. He too looked puzzled but still didn't speak.

By the way, up to now, the expedition had only cost the lives of two field mice - but a rabbit had had a close call as well due to Wilmer's misdirected arrow.

After a short rest, we attempted to retrace our steps, while thoughts of a meal of chips and sleeping in the tent filled our thoughts. Just as in all avenues of life when things are going along quite nicely, the unexpected happens. Suddenly, we were engulfed in low cloud.

"Keep together lads, try to walk at this angle!" said Shebe, gesticulating rapidly and speaking in a low, frightened voice.

40

As we walked, my mind drifted to the story my dad had recalled from his wartime years, whilst serving in the Eighth Army in Egypt. After a night out in Cairo, Dad and two other men were walking back to camp which was only two or three hundred yards into the desert. However, after ten minutes or so they realised not only were they lost but had been walking in circles. He maintained that it was only by chance that they'd stumbled on their camp.

My next thought was - are *we* walking in circles? And after that - are we still together? A quick check later and I could see that in fact, yes, we were. I told the boys to make sure that we didn't drift apart. The next 20 or 30 minutes passed and still the low cloud prevented us from seeing anymore than ten feet in front of us. I asked the boys if anybody knew where we were, or how far we were away from the valley? In reply there was deep silence - not a sound from anyone. It seemed probable that they were all wondering - as indeed was I - whether we were going to get back to camp before darkness fell.

"It's this way!"
"What?" I replied
"It's this way." De Silento of all people broke our fearful silence. And again, "It's this way, Dobbin."
"How do you know, De Silento?"
"I can remember that ground over there. If we walk on just a bit we will see the milestone that says two miles to Helmshore."
"Ok, De Silento, we'll try it. Blimey! He's right! It is there! He's right, yippee!"

We passed the source of the stream as we descended the moors, and in a fairly bright sunlight our little camp came into view. It was a relief to us all when our campfire began to roar. Our meal

41

was the next thing on our minds and half an hour later we were enjoying chips!

When dusk came, we tried to settle down for the night. However, our worn-out threadbare blankets were quite inadequate for what was a very chilly night in early spring. Once the fire dyed down, the temperature dropped even further. We had chatted and sung earlier on but now we struggled to stop our teeth from chattering. Morning couldn't come soon enough, and as soon as there was a little light we collected wood and started the fire. Then of course, we had to finish off the jam butts!

During that morning, our group just sat around our fire in relative silence - we had all turned into De Silento! That evening, on our return home, it was early to bed and we sure didn't need any rocking to sleep!

Frank Grey

Whilst on a sightseeing visit to view my childhood home after a time lapse of 50 years, I walked down the two miles of access road - this being the only way to reach the small hamlet where I was born and grew up. I passed an area at the side of the road where the large textile mill (long demolished) had stood. Only the mill workers cottages still stand which are now all privately owned. The mill had been built with its back up against a rock face. This was, in fact, the quarry which had supplied the stone for the mill and workers cottages.

As I stood looking at the small terraced cottage which had been my home for 20 years, memories came flooding back. In particular, the small corner shop (now a private house) from which my dad bought me penny sweets - mainly on the Fridays - as that was his pay day. Oh, and by the way my name is Frank - Frank Grey.

My nick name was Owerdy (all the male kids had nick names). Unfortunately, mine came about because of a rhyme that went 'Owerdy cowardly custard'. I was the youngest member of the gang - the runt if you will - because I was scrawny.

The sound of a steam train's whistle jolted me from my musing. I turned to see Puffing Billy steaming along the track which ran parallel to the cottages. The line is now operated by the East Lancashire Preservation Society. However, back when I was a child, British Rail ran the line and Puffing Billy would pull one small carriage up and down the 15 miles from the market town of Bury, to the end of the line at Bacup. Bacup is a small town at the foot of the Pennine Hills. Coal mining, textiles and boot and shoe manufacture were its main economic activity.

When the little train was out of earshot and lost in a cloud of smoke and steam, I walked over to a stone-built wall and just managed to look over with my chin resting on the cold stone. On the other side was the River Irwell which travelled from its source on the hills above Bacup, 30 miles to join the Manchester ship canal and then on to the sea at Liverpool. Looking at the river as it is now with clear clean water (and even some fish!) is a far cry from the polluted jet-black water that I knew as a child. At that time, industries throughout the length of the river were allowed to deposit almost anything into the water.

In my mind's eye, I can still see myself and the other boys wading out to stand on the small pebble islands which appeared when water levels were low. I would even try to encourage other people to paddle along with us. I can also visualize the stone throwing fights that we had across the river against the boys from Chatterton. Small boys can be very cruel, but I seemed more so than my friends - I had the devil in me!

I turned again from the river wall to look at the small area of land that stretched from the gable ends of the two rows of terraced houses. As I was saying, at one end had been the only shop in the hamlet. In the years that I lived there it was run by an elderly widow called Lorna Shaw. At times we would make her life a misery - and myself in particular! I would enter the shop just to ask for a 'broken spanish' (a liquorice stick only costing a penny) or simply to give cheek.

The spare land running from the shop gable to the river wall was our cricket and football pitch. Once, when playing catches with a hard cricket ball, I threw it to at a quiet boy we called De Silento. The ball hit him on the head. He went down for a few minutes. He never seemed the same after that. I must admit though, I did throw that ball hard and didn't expect him to catch it.

44

Later, as I got a little older I graduated into shoplifting. At first, just a few penny sweets. Later, I noticed that Lorna, the shopkeeper, returned quickly to the rear room of the shop after serving a customer, sometimes before they had even left. So, I had the idea that if I took my time to leave after buying sweets etc. and opened the door as if to leave, Lorna would retire to the rear lounge room. I would then jump over the counter, open the cash drawer and remove a few pennies. As time went by, I graduated onto shillings and then ten shillings and sometimes even pounds. I was very lucky not to get caught. I must have been very hard as I didn't feel at all guilty. However, as I grew into an adult I regretted that time in my life.

As I stood by the side of Lorna's shop door looking down the street, I had to blink a couple of times because in the distance two people were walking towards me. As they got about 20 yards away I thought to myself that I must be seeing things.   But no, it really was Mum and Dad. I smiled at them and they stretched out their arms in welcome and smiled back: broad, shining, lovely smiles. Come to think of it, I can't ever remember them smiling during my entire lifetime...

"Oh Doctor!"
"Yes, Nurse Heaton."
"Mr Grey has just opened his eyes for a brief moment."
"Yes Nurse, It's the first time I have ever seen any kind of movement during his entire two-year stay here in a coma"
"Mum and Dad it's not possible, you can't..."
"Nurse Heaton."
"Yes, Doctor Whitehead"
"Mr Grey has passed away."
"Oh Doctor, Mr Grey's son Arthur has just arrived."
"I will speak to him, Nurse!"

Arthur arrives by his father's bedside, tears glistening in his large pale eyes. The doctor turns to him with a look of deepest sympathy.

'Arthur, I'm very sorry to have to inform you that your father has passed away just moments ago."

Wiping a tear away, Arthur nods his head thoughtfully, "Oh, I know I shouldn't be surprised, but I still held out hope that he would eventually come out of the coma... and to think he sustained that head injury doing what he enjoyed the most, watching cricket. The man who was sat next to my dad said that he had never seen a ball hit as hard as the one that hit my dad on the head."

Status Quo

Two men are talking in a large office with dark oak panel wainscoting from floor to ceiling and mahogany parquet flooring. Long, Georgian sash windows allow the morning light to pour in to the room. One man sits with his back to the light in his leather recliner wingback chair, legs crossed, his blue, pinstripe suit clashing horribly with his spotted, mustard bow tie. The other man, sitting with rapt attention is on a similar chair, his chin balanced thoughtfully between forefinger and thumb. The first man taps his pipe onto an amber glass ashtray and clears his throat.

"Humph, Dennis!"
"Yes Colin."
"I made a big mistake in buying this Type R."
"How's that? I thought you liked the last one?"
"Yes I did but I've been very disappointed with this new series."
"Why?"
"Where do I start? It has a hopelessly bad ride, the handling has been compromised due to the absence of independent suspension, plus it's a heavier car. Even so, it only has a very marginal increase in power: one horsepower in fact... I could go on."
There is a polite knock at the door opposite Colin. "Yes, come in," intones Colin. A small, bespectacled lady with a timid, round face pokes her head around the door and quietly mumbles.

"Professor Ormiston."
"Yes, Miss Robinson."
"Bishop Monsignor Middleton has arrived."
"Thank you, will you direct him to my study?"

Rising from his chair Professor Ormiston, indicates politely towards the door:
 "Excuse me, Dennis."
"Colin! You have an unusual visitor - I mean this being a scientifically oriented establishment."
"Yes Dennis, but it's a personal matter regarding my son's education. The Bishop's in the area and I asked him to meet me here."
Without further ado Dennis rises, turning smartly to leave through the door behind him. Professor Ormiston remains standing to welcome his new guest. A man of medium height with grey-shot receding black locks wearing a black clerical waistcoat and traditional white collar strolls through the doorway. Professor Ormiston moves forward to greet his new guest with a rapid hand shake before reclining once more into his chair. He indicates for the bishop to sit also.

"Welcome Bishop, how should I address you during our meeting?"
"Please refer to me as Monsignor."
"Thank you Monsignor. I have been looking forward to our meeting for some time."
"As have I Professor Ormiston."
"As you are aware Monsignor, my son, Anthony is studying at Stoneyhurst College. However, as you also know, the matter I want to discuss with you is not related to him. As I indicated in my letter, I have asked you to meet me to gain your opinion on what we have discovered about the brain's reaction in our latest breakthrough brain scanning technique."
"Professor Ormiston, what interest is that to me, apart from in passing?"
"Monsignor, when I explain to you, I think you will be much more interested. For good reason, I didn't mention my main reason for inviting you here today. I am the only person who

knows the complete facts of what I am about to disclose to you, and before I inform the government, or proceed with publishing the paper, I first wanted to speak to you, due to your long experience in matters of faith."

"Professor Ormiston, I was under the impression that this establishment was only interested in scientifically proven medical procedures, and not matters of the heart and soul should we say?"

"That is true Monsignor, however, can I speak to you in layman's terms for a moment? As everyone knows, the human brain is the most complex computer on Earth, and most people realize we are a long way from understanding many aspects of that which we are currently investigating."

"Yes, Professor Ormiston."

"Monsignor, have you ever played a sport?"

"Yes, many years ago, but how can my playing sport be anything remotely relevant to our meeting?"

"Monsignor, when you played a sport, did you ever experience the sensation I am about to describe? I played cricket, and whilst fielding in particular, I have at times stopped a ball which has been fiercely hit, but I did it before I made a conscious decision to do so."

"Yes Professor, I have done the same when defending a parry whilst playing badminton."

"Quite so, Monsignor. However, we dismiss these sensations out of hand."

"Go on, Professor."

"Monsignor, through using a cutting-edge brain scanning technique which I developed at our laboratories here, and long and exhaustive investigation, I have proved beyond reasonable doubt that the human brain makes the decision six seconds before the person consciously knows what choice they are going to make!"

"What are you saying Professor, do you mean we are not in control of our own minds?"

"Not only that Monsignor, the findings also detect very accurately when the subject is asked to lie."

"Professor, regarding your first point, if I understand correctly, the subject's brain has decided its response prior to the person consciously knowing what choice they were going to make."

"Yes Monsignor."

"Professor, are you therefore saying that that the human being is simply a conduit, that the human mind simply witnesses what is being expressed?"

"To be blunt, yes that is in effect what I am saying."

"Professor, if we are to assume this theory is correct, what would you suspect is the nature of this - for want of a better word, 'force' - that pushes its way through us, deciding our reactions?"

"Monsignor, I am positive that there are in fact 'forces'."

"Forces!"

"Yes, more than one."

"Well, how many?"

"Two."

"Two in one person?"

"No, Monsignor, only one in each person, I have found two distinctive forces."

"What are you saying professor? Good and Evil?"

"Yes Monsignor, the forces we call God and the Devil."

"Professor, are you sure you will be able to detect each?"

"Yes, it will be quite easily done. As you know, we don't need a scanner to detect basic love or hate. We can see the force we call love as it is used to comfort our family and friends, and it's plain to see. But it's not as easy to see evil, especially when it's in a pseudo-loving embrace, or a lie from the tongue of a politician. However, it's quite easy to detect these things using my methods. Also, Monsignor, this technology will make it quite possible in the near future to develop, amongst other things, a lie detector with absolute precision. Where the truth is paramount, crime, loyalty etc., I predict that this tool will be able to run a check on anyone, say in public life - a politician, the police, newspaper editors and owners."

"Professor, you are sure that no one could possibly evade being found out?"

"Monsignor, the beauty of the test is that it can uncover the true thoughts in a person's brain before they could consciously modify them."

"Professor, should these methods be put into practice, they will have far reaching consequences. The world will be changed dramatically. And as for the point about the existence of dual forces which you have apparently scientifically measured for the first time - these findings could at last prove what many people have believed for thousands of years! - Professor Ormiston, do you mind if I ask you a personal question?"

"No, not all Monsignor."

"Do you have a faith in your life to which you have a devout belief?"

"Yes, I am a Christian. Monsignor, I would like to draw our meeting to an end as I feel I can't elaborate any further, but I will look forward very much to your thoughts on these subjects. I realize there has been a lot of information to take in. Thank you for listening."

"Professor Ormiston, I have never felt quite the way I feel at this moment. Even though the day I was ordained as a priest many years ago was a very special day, I feel that today is equally momentous. Professor Ormiston, can I ask you to please refrain, for the time being at least, from divulging any of the contents of our conversation until I speak to you again after I have had time to digest all this stunning information.

"Yes Monsignor. I can't see a few days making any difference as I have been working for many years on these findings."

Two days pass, another man sits in a wainscotted office much like the first one.   He is behind a wooden desk and is writing something in a large leather-bound book. The phone next to him rings once and he answers.

"Doctor Thatcher."
"Yes Miss Robinson."
"Have you seen Professor Ormiston this morning?"
"No, Miss Robinson."
"That's strange. He hasn't phoned in. He usually does if he's been held up in any way."
"Professor Ormiston hasn't missed a day's work in the last 39 years, Miss Robinson."
"Yes Doctor Thatcher."
"Have you tried phoning his home?"
"Not as yet, because he would always call here."
"Well, I think we will risk his wrath Miss Robinson; phone his home right away please."
"Yes, right away Doctor."

Behind the large oak doors of an old, immaculately presented Georgian mansion another phone rings.
"Good morning, Professor Ormiston's residence."
"Oh! Good morning, this is Miss Robinson speaking. I am Professor Ormiston's secretary."
"Good morning Miss Robinson, this is Detective Sergeant Knowles. I'm afraid I have some very bad news for you. Professor Ormiston has been killed in a terrible car crash this morning. I am very sorry."

Doctor Thatcher enters Miss Robinson's office concern written across his face in deep etches on his brow. He is almost completely bald except for the odd tuft here and there. He has a big bushy brown moustache and kind brown eyes.

"Miss Robinson – are you alright?"

"No Doctor Thatcher, I am not and I don't think I will ever be the same again. Doctor Thatcher, would you mind if I return home? I can't carry out my duties today."

"Of course Miss Robinson, I understand. It's been a terrible shock, especially for you."

"Thank you Doctor, I will see you tomorrow."

"Yes, Miss Robinson."

Miss Robinson is sitting behind a big oak desk in her office. The grey light weakly penetrates Georgian windows opposite but fails to lighten the hanging gloom. Her phone rings once.

"Miss Robinson."

"Yes."

"We have a Detective Sergeant Knowles at reception. He would like to speak to you."

"Please send him up. Thank you."

Sergeant Knowles knocks and enters Miss Robinson office. He is a small squat fellow wearing leather gloves and a long beige raincoat. Miss Robinson turns around in her chair and rises to greet him.

"Good morning Miss Robinson."

"Good morning Sergeant."

"Miss Robinson, would it be possible to speak to Doctor Thatcher? Is he available?"

"One moment, I will check with him."

Miss Robinson picks up her phone and pushes four buttons. The phone at the other end is answered quickly. "Doctor Thatcher, Sergeant Knowles is here. Are you able to come over to speak with him? Five minutes, yes ok." She nods before replacing the handset and turning back towards the sergeant. "Yes he is Sergeant and will be with us shortly."

"Miss Robinson. I have some information regarding the tragic accident."

"Yes Sergeant."

"We now know that Professor Ormiston died instantly when the car he was driving was in a collision with a motorway bridge support."

"Sergeant, I can't understand how that could have happened. He was a brilliant driver. Only recently, he had been driving a Ferrari whilst on holiday in the Lake District."

"I'm sure he was Miss Robinson, however we do have a witness who I feel is reliable. It is a priest, Father Wilfred O'Neil. He was following not far behind Professor Ormiston's Type 'R'. He saw the vehicle veer wildly from the overtaking lane to the nearside lane, then into the bridge support at what must have been eighty miles an hour. The tyre marks on the road are also very apparent."

"Excuse me Sergeant, I will just let Doctor Thatcher in."

Doctor Thatcher enters, wearing a pale, drawn expression.
"Good morning Sergeant."

"Doctor, can I offer my condolences for the sad loss of your esteemed colleague."

"Thank you Sergeant."

"Doctor Thatcher, I must ask you, were you aware of any sensitive information which Professor Ormiston might have had with him at the time of his death, regarding patients etc.?"

"No Sergeant, I wasn't privy to any of Professor Ormiston's work and studies related to brain scanners. I deal with, shall we say, more mundane procedures and the patient's files are stored on the main computer."

"Where did Professor Ormiston keep his data etc.?"

"It was stored on his laptop and he had that with him at all times. Sergeant, why are you so interested in the Professor's work?"

"Oh no, it's not that Doctor Thatcher, it's just that there was a laptop in his car."

"Sergeant, please, it must be returned to the lab at once."

"I'm sorry Doctor; it was destroyed completely in the crash."

"Oh dear Lord! I was always saying to Colin, err I mean Professor Ormiston, we should duplicate all our related work as we do with the NHS files."

"Yes, Doctor that is always a good principle to adhere to."

Miss Robinson takes a week or so off work, attends the funeral of Professor Ormiston, but realizes that she must return to work to tie up some loose ends. She is sitting at her desk looking dazed and withdrawn when Doctor Thatcher enters wearing a sympathetic smile.

"Miss Robinson."

"Yes Doctor Thatcher."

"I didn't get the chance to speak to you at Colin's funeral, but I would just like to say how sad I was for Colin's son, especially as it is, as you know, only a year since he lost his mother - Colin's wife Judith - to a brain tumour. And I know you were very close to Colin as a work colleague for, I believe, thirty-nine years."

"Yes Doctor Thatcher, to be honest I have been devastated and I feel I must consider my future regarding my continuing on at the lab."

"I understand. Oh, Miss Robinson."

"Yes Doctor Thatcher."

"I hope at this distressing time that the haste of this move is not seen as unduly callous but Colin's replacement is to be announced at this week's staff meeting."

"Do you know who it is Doctor?"

"Yes I do. It's a man I have heard of. I believe he is a very well respected and brilliant professor."

"What is his name?"

"He's called Professor Christian O'Neil."

The Winding Room

Winding Room n. - the room in a cotton mill where yarn, brought from the spinning room, is prepared for use in the weaving process

"Doctor Who, is he Chinese?"

"No Dad, it's just a name."

"Just a name?"

"Yes, it's a new series on BBC, this is the first episode."

"Why can't they put something decent on at teatime, like *The Grove Family*?"

"Oh Dad, young people want something new and modern, not one of those kitchen sink dramas."

"Your mother likes the Groves."

"I know Dad."

"Mildred! Come here. Just look at this new programme that's on."

"Just a minute Joe, I'm ironing Raymond's shirt."

"Raymond, where are you off to tonight?"

"We're going to the *Nelson Imperial*."

"Raymond, why don't you stay in some weekends?"

"Oh Dad, people don't stay in nowadays."

"I know, but it's not a good thing. I don't want you coming home drunk, it upsets your mother. And no fighting this week; I don't want you coming home covered in blood like last week."

"Right Dad, but that wasn't my fault. I'd only gone to the gents and this lad said I was staring at him. He said, 'What are you staring at,' and I said, 'I don't know, there isn't a label on it.' Then it all kicked off."

Mildred breaks off ironing and comes over. "What is it Joe?"

"Mildred, it's this new programme, Doctor Who."

"Doctor Who?"

"Yes, and don't say is he Chinese, 'Cos he's not."
"Joe, who thinks these stupid programmes up? I can't see it lasting very long, people won't watch it."
"Mother, don't start saying things like that when Jack comes in."
"Raymond!"
"What?"
"Remember what I told you the other night"
"No, what?"
"Don't be bothering with any good looking women. Look for a plain girl. If you get a good looking girl there will be always be blokes after her."
"Oh Dad, chance would be a fine thing."
"And remember, Raymond, no Catholics or you'll end up with a house full of kids."
"You've some room to talk! Me, youngest of eleven kids!"
"Precisely! I'm only trying to help you lad."
"Ok Dad, when I ask a bird to dance, I'll say, 'Oh by the way, what religion are you?'"
"Raymond!"
"Yes Mum."
"Your tea's ready."
"Ok Mum, coming."

They all sit down to eat at a big wooden table in the dining room. The unmistakable aroma of tripe and onions fills the air. Raymond's father and mother tuck in heartily, whereas Raymond picks at his tripe with a faint frown on his face.

"Dad, do you never get fed up of tripe and onions"
"No never lad. I've got one of the best jobs in't world as well. I've worked in't tripe shop for over 40 years."
"Yes Dad, but tripe and onions every day for tea seems a bit strange to me."
"Nothing of the sort Raymond, this is proper grub."

Then they all eat in silence until all the tripe is eaten. As they eat Raymond's father glows with satisfaction and health; Raymond starts to look a little green around the gills. Suddenly, there is a knock at the front door, Mildred goes to answer it.

"Raymond! Jack's here."
"Ok Mum. Hiya Jack!"
"Ok Ray?"
"Yes, just trying to digest my tripe tea."
"Tripe again Ray!"
"What have you had?"
"A pork pie."
"Jammy devil."
"Is your car running ok, Jack?"
"Yes, touch wood."
"Touch my dad's head will you? Ha-ha!"
"Jack, we don't want a night like last Saturday, do we?"
"Bloody hell, no. When that hose came undone and we lost all the water from the engine! No joke!"
"And I had to knock on that front door and ask for a bucket of water."
"Come on Ray, let's get going."
"Drive carefully, Jack."
"Ok, Mrs O'Malley."
"First stop the *White Lion*, Jack."
"Yes Ray, a few pints of Red Barrel."

Ray and Jack leave the house and get in Jack's green Morris Minor. Jack turns the key and they are off on their Friday night adventure. They drive to Jack's house, park up and walk the rest of the way to the *White Lion*. They soon see an ornate Victorian building set at the end of row of terraced shops that uses an overlooking turret topped by a short minaret to round the corner to its other side. It has three tall chimneys and *White*

59

Lion proudly signposted on both sides of the building next to the roof in gold lettering. The friends go inside and start to sink one pint after another chatting all the while.

"Sound Jack. It's strange, although I've had four pints I still feel thirsty."
"Yes, weird, I do as well."
"We'll have two more, then it's to *The Imp*."
"Ray, let's have a change next Saturday, shall we?"
"Aye, we could try *The Astoria* in Rawtenstall."
"Ok."

They continue to drink a few more pints and have a good laugh taunting and teasing one another while casually looking around the room now and again to admire one or two graceful female forms. At one point, Ray plucks up courage and goes over to talk to one girl who is out with her mates. She is a good looking girl with blond curly hair tumbling to her shoulders and smiling blue eyes. He returns shortly to continue talking to Jack.

"Not been a bad night Ray."
"No not bad, Jack. What's on your mind you look a bit down?"
"I know, in a way, we have a decent job at the mill, but I don't look forward to Mondays do you?"
"Do I heck! That bloody Winding Room, all that noise. It's almost as noisy as *The Imp*, ha-ha! But I know what you mean, and that bloke Bernard, what a strange man!"
"Yeah, what a Mary Anne. I don't know how long I can stand it to be honest, I've been thinking about going down south and trying to get work in the holiday industry, what about you Ray?"
"I don't know Jack; I can't see any alternative for me. I suppose I'll follow the same path as my brothers and sisters, get married and have kids."

"Yes Ray, your family's made a big contribution to the population explosion hasn't it?"

"Thanks Jack, you are very understanding, you sarcastic git!"

"Sorry Ray."

"Jack, that bird I was talking to tonight, well I think she's not the usual type; I mean she has such a gentle stare. I think she might be the one."

"Blimey Ray, you've only just met her!"

"I know, but I've noticed her before when she was with another bloke. She's not seeing him now, however."

"When are you seeing her again?"

"Tomorrow night, we're going to the Odeon in Burnley."

"What's on?"

"It's a film called, *Saturday Night and Sunday Morning*."

"Ray, is she paying?"

"No, I might pay for this one."

"What's her name?"

"She's called Bernadette."

It is back to the dreaded Monday morning grind and Ray goes to work as usual at the Cotton Mill in the area known as the Winding Room. The mill is a massive brick built, three-storey building with a tall round chimney standing proud by at least the height of the factory again. Ray braces himself as he enters the building and goes to the Winding Room. This is the room where the cotton yarn is taken from the spinners bobbins and prepared for weaving. It is accomplished by 'winding machines'. They do this by either winding it on to warp beams (a roller at the back of the loom) or on to pirns that fit into the shuttle on the weaving machine. The beams provide the warp of the finished cloth. The shuttle travels across the warp threads, providing the weft. Due to the sheer number of winding machines the noise in the room is deafening. Ray isn't at his machine long before he spies Bernard approaching who bellows at him in order to be heard.

"Blinking heck Raymond, you're in on time! And no black eyes! Have you stayed in this weekend?"

"You must be joking Bernard, I was out Saturday and Sunday."

"It's about time you settled down."

"Yes I might do that, and sooner than you think."

"Bernard!" Bernard turns round to face Jack, who is a tall willowy man with a blackened face and ginger hair.

"What Jack?"

"We've got a cotton waste fire!"

"Where?"

"It's in Number One Winding Frame."

"Right, bring the tools and the extinguisher."

"Right."

Jack grabs the extinguisher and runs off with Bernard; before shortly returning for the rest of the tools. He departs again with redoubled haste. Ray continues to work steadily until lunch time. As he finishes off his work he looks over to Jack coming towards him, wiping the sweat from his brow.

"Phew! What a morning Ray."

"Too right, Jack; brew time. I think we've earned it. Give us one of your butties Jack."

"How's it you haven't got one of your own?"

"I left them on the kitchenette."

"It's not like you that Ray. Ok, here you are, I don't know if I can stand this job much longer, it's more like a prison than a prison."

"How do you know? You've never been to prison."

"I know, but you know what I mean, and that Bernard's had a right pop at me this morning."

"I know Jack, but he has all the responsibility in this room, and if he sees you squirting our new apprentice with your oil can, what do you expect?"

"You've changed your tune, Ray. It's not long ago that you were squaring up to him."

"I know Jack, but it can't be easy for him; if these machines are not producing he gets it in the neck."

"I suppose you're right; I know it's not his fault. I'm just not happy at my work. I think I'll give a week's notice and try my luck down south."

"What, just get in the car and go?"

"Yeah, I think so."

"Anyway Ray, how did you go on last night? Was it a good film, or did you not see much of it? You know what I mean!"

"I saw most of it thank you very much."

"That's not like you, Ray."

"I've never been as bad as most people seem to think, but I'm a changed man."

"It certainly looks like it. This bird, is she a Burnley girl?"

"Yes."

"What's her name?"

"Bernadette."

"What's her second name?"

"It's O'Tool."

"O'Tool! Not Bernard's daughter?"

"Yes."

"Does he know?"

"No, but he will do tonight. I'm going round to his house."

"What for?"

"To ask for his daughter's hand in marriage."

New Career

Whilst eating my 'tatie' scones I started to think, and as I was trying to analyse a few conclusions, the main conclusion came to the fore! This being so, I feel the direction of my life has to change in order to fulfil my heart's desire. A second conclusion immediately came to mind. If I could take steps to try to implement the actions which would have to occur, could I deal with the consequences? The third conclusion then arrived: should I just accept my lot and conclude that my life, like many others, will never be content – in an emotional sense at least. However, I feel I have a destiny to fulfil, some special role in life waiting for me, the same kind of force which compelled me to do a job like this, a job almost nobody else would do.

As I sat pondering, a voice behind me shocked me from my trance.

"Robin! Are you going to sit there all night? We still have two streets in Stoneyholme that need their middens emptying."

"Alright Jack, I'll be with you in a sec."

As I reached for my number 16 shovel, I briefly thought about my workmate Jack Hatfield. His life is infinitely more severe in the sense that his home life must be very trying. Eight children under the age of ten, and he has lost his wife to TB – yet I never hear him moaning or complaining about the hard work. In fact, he is, I know, very thankful to have his council job.

"Jack, I'll be glad when they connect these streets up to the main sewers."

"I won't Robin, I need this job; where would I get another that pays three pounds a week? If I went back into the mill I'd be lucky to get one pound ten shillings a week."

"That's right Jack; I'm just being selfish. As you know, I've been saving up during the last few years of doing this night work in order to pay for a fulltime education, amongst other things."

"Yes, what did you say you wanted to do when you get the qualification?"
 "I want to get a job on the Burnley Express as a journalist."
"Blimey Robin, that's better than having to work for your living!"
"Yes, Jack, I know what you mean."
"Robin, if you get a job on't paper, would it make you think about me still doing this and knowing where the papers end up. Ha-ha!"
"Too right Jack. I only hope people read it first."
"Well Robin, they won't be reading it after!"
"Robin, I'm not trying to pry on you or owt but what's happening, if anything with that lass you were keen on?"
"There's nothing happening, Jack. I still have feelings for Nurse O'Neill but it's a difficult situation. Anyway Jack, don't worry about me, you have enough on your plate. I don't know how you keep your spirits up."
"I do that at the Corporation Arms, Robin. Ha-ha!"

It is a slow night, a real grind. Anyway, as we work away I have a sudden thought. "Jack! Drive down Market Street tonight; I just want to look in the window at Pollard's shop."
"Alright Robin, but what for?"
"Oh, I just want to look at a guitar that's in there. I've been saving up for a new one for about two years."
"It's a strange thing to want to play in't it Robin? I like a good brass band. Queen's Park grandstand on a Sunday, you can't beat it."
"Well Jack, it's my Irish ancestry that draws me to folk music."

We look in at Pollard's -the old pawnbrokers - and see a sky-blue guitar glistening in the window beneath the street lights, and an intense yearning overtakes me. I force myself to look away but something draws my gaze back again.

"Ah, yes Robin, it's a fine bit of wood that, what will that cost you?"

"Oh, about three pounds."

"Three pounds! Blimey Robin."

After I spend a minute or two more mooning at the guitar in the shop window, we return to our grind, or should I say grime? Just as I banish all musical dreams from my mind, I spot something in the night sky.

"That's strange, Jack."

"What do you mean, Robin?"

"No, look Jack. That light in the sky above Pollard's shop."

"Oh, yes. I think it's the moon."

"No Jack, the moon's in its first quarter, and it's over there, and the moon doesn't move - or not so the human eye would notice. No Jack, whatever it is, it's moving."

"I think you're right. Come on Robin; let's get back to the depot."

"No Jack, we'll have to watch it. I'm intrigued. It's the strangest sight I've ever seen."

"Robin! It has two colours, no three - blue, tinged with a lighter blue, and a deep claret. It's lower than it was and it's moving over towards the canal. Get in the wagon, we'll follow it."

"Right Jack. Hey Jack, I hope we don't get the sack when we bring this wagon back."

"That's a bit of poetry Robin."

"Yes Jack. Wait, it's over Fitzpatrick's Temperance Bar."

"Has it stopped?"

"No Jack, it's still moving."

"Is it one of those Zeppelins Robin?"

"Is it heck Jack. Jack! It's moving towards Turf Moor, the football stadium of Burnley FC Its landing! Quick, drive the wagon under the canal bridge; I want to get a closer look at it."

"Don't get out Robin!"

"I've got to Jack."

"Why? Are you mad?"
"Come back Robin, don't go near it. The light is blinding."
"I don't know why I'm drawn like a moth to a flame, I suppose.
I'm sorry Jack, I know you can't hear me, I can't explain. I just
have this overwhelming compulsion to go to the lights."

What happened next I am not sure; I just remember the light
getting brighter and brighter until I could see nothing else...
 And then when I looked down I saw my body, feet, legs, hips and
then stomach also being consumed by the light. There was a
blinding flash and then...

I now have no conscious sense of time or space; just the feeling
of company, and a kind of remote communication - it's like part
living in a human sense but in a different sphere. Whatever I am
I have no idea; all I can say or think is that I will return.   At
times, I think about my workmate, Jack Hatfield, and what he
must have said when he took the wagon back to the depot –
having to say Robin Coyle has gone to heaven in a claret and
blue star!

The Cellar Under Greenmount

Gordon and David are two old friends having a night out in a pub, pretending that they are young men again. They are deeply engrossed in conversation...

"Having time to think is denied to the majority of people unless one is in full-time education. Even these people are not really thinking in an inward way. Studying one or two subjects only trains the mind into a narrow field, and if people are in fulltime work it's not possible to find time to think, especially people with children. Adults, in fact, don't make many constructive decisions through thinking over a long period of time. Most have their minds made up for them when watching adverts on TV or the internet. Until recently, tabloid newspapers would back one particular political party, ensuring they would be elected. People don't seem to realize the only interest these newspapers really have is to make money."
"Yes, that might be right to a certain degree, but we talk over a drink and seem to reach independent decisions about many subjects."
"I know, but when we are drinking we are not thinking realistically. When tomorrow comes we will not remember anything we discussed."
"What about when we talk sport, we always remember those discussions."
"Yes, we seem to, but we always talk about the same team!"
"I know, what do you think about the people who don't like sport?"
"Well, unless they are into what we wouldn't call sport, like shooting or fishing, I would say they have started to evolve into another species!"

"Blimey! Yes, like that Scottish lad on that TV programme, *Mock the Week*. His only interest is himself."

"Yes, none of the others can get a word in. I think the bald-headed lad is the only naturally funny guy."

"What do you think about the talk of the risk of power cuts being possible in the next two years?"

"I think we should invest more money into wind farms."

"Some people who are against having more of them say producing them creates a very large carbon footprint. But at least they produce energy unlike private cars or articulated wagons."

"Yes, but we will need thousands!"

"Well, we've got plenty of land which the vast majority of people will never see during their lifetime."

"Hey, did you hear that joke?"

"Let's hear it."

"This kid went to his pals for a sleepover. When he came home the next day he said to his mum, 'Mum, what is it called when someone sleeps on top of someone?' His mum thought for a minute before deciding to tell him the truth- 'It's called having sex.'

'Oh,' said the kid.

When we went to school the next day he told his pal what his mum had said. The next day when the kid arrived home from school he approached his mum.

'Hey Mum! It's called bunk beds! And my pal's mum wants a word with you!'"

"Ha-ha! Very funny, are we having another or what?"

"Aye, we'll just have one more, I'll get them."

"Blimey! You're letting your hair down, what's brought this on?"

"Don't know, it must be the drink in me."

The night moved on and the two companions continue to drink taking it in turns to buy them. The conversation begins to steadily degenerate...

"That tastes good, you can't beat Fosters."

"I know, I could drink a bucket full!"

"You have done."

"Hey look! She's in again."

"Yes, I'd noticed, she's got a fair top-set on her."

"Oh, I hadn't noticed them."

"Bloody liar."

"No, but you've had a lot of women haven't you?"

"No comment."

"No, we all know which type of women are the best, you know, up for it."

"Well, if we are going to bring our conversation down to this level. The best are the selfish women. Just think about it, an unselfish woman is far too unselfish."

"Yes, I hadn't thought about it in that way before."

"They've got a band on in here at weekend."

"Aye, who is it?"

"Biglicks."

"Oh I might come in, they cover some of Pink Floyd's stuff."

"Yeah, they've been around for donkey's years. If you're a musician, it's usually for life."

"Yes, life should mean life."

"Oh, don't start on about that old chestnut."

"Ok."

"Did you read that in the local paper?"

"What?"

"The oldest veteran from the First World War has died."

"Yes."

"When you think about it we're still a very basic animal aren't we?"

"Yes, we are only at the dawn of civilization, I wonder if we will live, you know, as a species till the twilight."
"I don't know, but we don't understand much about the human brain, or mind as we call it. The experts say the human mind is so complex it will eventually create a solution to any person's problem; but then it may kill them in the process..."

One or two drinks later...
"I think we'll just have a brandy then we'll get going."
"Aye, ok."
I don't want to get you into trouble, you know, with the wife."
"No, she's the unselfish type – ha-ha."
"Yeah, I thought she was; only kidding."
"Right, let's go. Which way are we going home?"
"Have we to get a taxi?"
"No, too expensive, we'll walk."
"Tight get!"
"Well, I think if we're serious about getting fit, we should make a start tonight."
"Yeah right, after six pints of Fosters and two brandies!"
"We're still walking. It's only three miles."
"Ah, you're drunk, you're drunk you silly old fool."

One of the companions starts to make some sort of noise placed somewhere between a cat being strangled and a zombie being butchered.
"Oh, don't start singing; you have one of those voices."
"What do you mean?"
"Better lip-read than heard!"
"Ok, come on, let's make a start. If we take that short cut up Porrits Lane we can cut through the gardens where Greenmount used to stand."
"Right, you're not just a pretty face."
"No, just pretty ugly."

"Right, come on, first foot forward."

"Not been a bad night 'as it?"

"No, we'll have to do it more often."

"Yeah, we always say that don't we?"

"No, but this time we will."

"Yeah right."

"Just got to climb this little wall and sneak past the gate house and we'll be almost home."

"Yippee!"

"Shhh, you'll wake 'em up."

"They say there's still a wine cellar belonging to the big house somewhere around here."

"Aye, I've heard that, and it's still supposed to be full!"

Silence falls, for a moment. Gordon can hear a noise but in the sudden, total darkness beyond the gatehouse he cannot see David at all.

"Where are you, David?"

"I'm down here Gordon."

"Down where?"

"Have you got any matches? It's dark."

"It usually is at night."

"No, I'm in t'cellar."

David, squints downwards and just about makes out a patch of even darker blackness just to his left. He removes his matches from his trouser pocket and throws them towards the inky darkness.

"Here you go, catch!"

"Oops, dropped 'em!"

"Wait, I'm cummin' down."

"Ok, jump! I'll catch you."

72

"Ow! You fat get."
"Shut up and strike a match."
"Right, what can you see?"
"Nothing, it's empty!"

Frank Buttley

It was a quiet day at the factory. That might sound contradictory, but it was Saturday - and that meant that all the machinery was idle. The workmen who usually operated them were involved with cleaning or doing some maintenance work. Usually, it was almost impossible to have a conversation due to the deafening noise.

Alan and Herbert were chatting whilst renewing a tape belt on the spinning frame.

"Alan! Frank's trying to sell his car".

"Blimey Herbert! I thought he would never get rid of that car, ever!"

"I know, but he's decided to buy a new one. That 20 year old Ford of his looks 'as new' and Percy was telling me it's still on its original tyres. According to Percy, he bought it in 1946."

Alan chirped in, "I might try to buy it off him. I'll ask him how much he wants for it."

"Good luck to you, but you know what he's like. Yesterday he went to the office to complain because his wage was a penny short; he has a mind like a slide rule"

"Percy!" Herbert shouted across the room.

"What do you want Herbert?"

"Where's Frank?"

"He's gone over to the carding room; he says they have our oil can. You'd think it was his own property."

"Yeah!"

The sound of a trombone echoed in the stairway. Frank Buttley was on the way. He was middle-aged, of average height, and slightly balding. Frank wasn't the shrinking violet type: whenever the factory was silent he played his imaginary trombone. This was done with his mouth only, but it sounded just as bad as the real thing

"Frank!" Percy said, "Shut that racket!"

Frank ignored him, of course, and carried on 'tromboning'.
When he finally stopped playing he said, "I've got our oil can back Percy!"

"Ok Frank."

"Frank, we're brewing up are you having one?"

"I think I will Percy, has Alan and Herbert gone brewing?"

"Yes"

When they came back with their tin cups of tea, Alan, Herbert and Percy sat on the window ledge eating a butty. Frank went over to his two clothes-lockers and opened one of them. This locker was full to the brim with all manner of things – Frank was a magpie. When he rejoined the group he was holding in one hand a tin-opener and in the other, a can of food.

"What have you got for lunch today, Frank?" Herbert asked. In reality, he already knew that Frank didn't actually have a clue. (During the war Frank and his wife had run a grocers shop. They did so until about 1950 when they sold it. They had kept the shop's stock and were still using food from what must have been a full stock room.)

Frank was opening the can; most of them didn't have labels on. This one didn't have one either.

"What are you on today, Frank?" Herbert said again.

"Gooseberries."

Bloody hell Frank!" Herbert said, "I'm glad I've got this bacon butt, don't fancy yours at all."

As the lads were finishing their break, the supervisor came over to make sure they were working on the correct programme.

"Yeah Walt, we're on schedule."

Being able to come into work on a Saturday morning was a bonus that was only available to the men who had been on the early morning shift that week. They would then work until noon on Saturday. As finishing time arrived the men waited for the clock to strike 12 and then clocked off. Alan struck up a conversation with Frank.

"Is the car still for sale?"

"Yes, Alan, but I have to go to the car showroom this afternoon. I'm buying an Austin 1100."

"Blimey Frank! That will cost a packet."

"Too right Alan, £600!"

"What are you looking for the Ford, Frank?"

"About £100 Alan, but I might trade it in, it just depends."

"Frank, if I call on you Sunday morning will you know as I'm interested in it?"

"I should do Alan. Call in number 73, Bolton Road North."

"Ok Frank, I'll see you during Sunday morning."

Percy and Alan were stood waiting for the Haslingden bus.

"Alan," Percy said.

"Yes, what Percy."

"You've not know Frank very long, have you?"

"No, only about two years."

"Well, you know what a tight get he is?"

"Yeah Percy, tighter than a duck's backside!"

"Did you hear the tale when Frank was in the Auxiliary Fire Service during the war?"

"No, what happened?"

"One of the fire fighters went into Frank's shop, when he knew he was out and asked Frank's wife for four oranges, saying Frank sent him for them. When he got back to the fire station he shared them out with the men, including Frank. Frank only realized where the oranges had come from when he arrived home for tea. He wasn't happy at all!"

On Sunday morning Alan walked the six miles over to Frank's house in Ramsbottom. Finding the front door closed he gave it a knock. Frank eventually opened the door.

"Come in Alan."

"Mornin' Frank, thank you."

"Alan, did you see Herbert anywhere near my lockers yesterday?"

"No, why?"

"I'm sure he's been shaking them again. When I unlocked them yesterday everything was upset."

"Oh," said Alan, "I didn't see him do it."

"Anyway, come in Alan."

Alan walked into the terraced house. He entered a narrow hallway. As he walked down there were newspapers stacked up almost six feet high, all the way down. At the bottom of the hall there were two doors, one on the left which was the entrance to the front lounge. As the door was open, Alan glanced into this room on the way past. It was stacked high with various sized boxes. Alan was taken into the room at the rear. This had a small settee, an armchair and a small dining table with two chairs. Leading off this room was a small outkitchen. However, even this room was loaded with boxes; one of which was open. Alan glanced into it: it full of matchboxes. The rest of them were closed. Neither of the men mentioned anything regarding the unusual state of the place.

"How did you go on with the car Frank?"

"I'm sorry Alan I sold the car to the garage. The salesman made me a good offer and I took it."

"Ok Frank, never mind."

"Sorry Alan, sorry you've had to trail down here."

"See you tomorrow, Frank."

"Wait a minute Alan, I'll give you a lift home in the new motor."

"Thanks Frank."   Well I have to say, Alan thought, Frank's not as tight as he's been made out.

Coffee Break

It is just after lunch time in a concert hall in the heart of London. Two friends begin a conversation...

"Gordon!"

"Yes, what David? I'm busy just now."

"Just have a short break with me; I've got ten minutes before I have to get back to the grindstone."

"Alright David, pour me a cup of coffee will you old man? Thank you David."

"Gordon, did you spot our Miss Layfield?"

"No David, what do you mean?"

"Oh, don't start that 'holier than thou' attitude!"

"Well David, I did notice her - or shall I say I appreciated the rather striking figure."

"Yes Gordon, that's putting it mildly. I believe she has a younger sister with a terrific rear end!"

"Thank you David, can we change the tone of the conversation to a subject I have been thinking about recently?"

"Yes Gordon, carry on."

"David, who would have predicted, or even had an inkling, as to the immense changes we have made as a nation? Britain has changed beyond imagination from the 1940s and 50s, and now in the early years of the 21st century we have one of the most diverse communities in the world and an infrastructure that is comparable to any in Western Europe."

"Yes Gordon, that goes without saying, but some of the changes are quite sobering. For instance, who would have ever imagined that women would have become bigger, stronger, and have more tattoos than men."

"David, trust you to bring the subject around to women, even if they are the tattooed variety."

"Gordon, we always have to follow your line in any of our conversations. You are so pompous. I can't understand how you have accrued all this knowledge because I know you, unfortunately, failed the 11+ exam."

"Yes David, thank you for reminding me of that fact, however you omit to mention my four 'A' levels and my First Class Honours degree. Your education David, if we can call it one, was only due to 'daddy' having a very large wallet."

"Touché Gordon! Gordon, I must say your academic success is, of course, a credit to you. The work that must have been put in – plus a fair amount of determination goes without saying."

"Thank you , David."

"You're welcome. But Gordon, did you somehow find a way to cheat?"

"No, I didn't! But I believe some of the students found ways to do just that. The students of today don't need to cheat at all; the exams are designed so as most students are able to pass quite easily. However, David, I am impressed as it's not like you to put a bit of thought into, shall we say, 'The Establishment'!"

"And I promise I won't mention anything again that might interest you!"

"David, even if I don't sometimes show it, I do value your opinions, apart from when you are espousing the aesthetic contribution of tattooed women! But on a more serious note regarding education, I feel the vast majority of students are led into the wrong train of thought during their final years of schooling which renders them more or less useless to society or themselves and with minds which are managed, in the main, by tabloid newspapers or the commercial internet, or television stations, whose only interest is keeping the status quo."

"Yes Gordon, I suppose you are right as usual."

"Excuse me, Maestro!"

"Yes, Miss Layfield!"

"The orchestra's ready for the rehearsal, sir."

"I will be ready in five minutes. Thank you."

"What are you rehearsing today? David?"

"Oh Gordon! It's a beautiful piece of music, one of my favourite works -it's Sibelius' *Finlandia*."

"That's mine too."

"Are you staying on after work Gordon to enjoy this piece?"

"Yes, I will be here anyway for another couple of hours as I haven't finished cleaning the seats in the upper circle!"

Complicated Skies

In a plush office in London a gentleman and a lady are engaged in conversation.

"Why should the BBC try to compete with the commercial companies? It could leave all the trashy and rather common programmes to the commercial productions. Series like, *Spooks*, *Waterloo Road*, *Holby City*, *Eastenders*, *Casualty* etc. can all be seen in a slightly different guise on many other channels. This would save a great deal of money, money which the public wouldn't need to find. If these steps were taken it would allow the BBC to employ people who really wanted to work as public servants, indeed as many people do in local government or politics. This would allow most of the high earners to return to the commercial workplace where they belong."

"Yes I agree Albert; however, I think the BBC should employ people like Katie Price. She did a good job on, *I'm A Celebrity Get Me Out Of Here*. Not many people would have tried to chew a fish eye."

"Good grief Sandra! Sometimes I wonder how you managed to achieve the position of Health Authority Commissioner!"

"What do you mean Albert? You watched and enjoyed the programme."

"Yes I did, but I don't think being able to eat a fish eyeball qualifies somebody for a career in broadcasting."

""Albert, I know it might seem very unusual to you that a person can enjoy some entertainments or literature of a very trivial standard, but this fact doesn't mean that I can't put my academic head on when required."

"I do realize this Sandra, and you are very able in your chosen career, it's just that of late my patience has been quite short."

A change of scene; some weeks later an intimate scene unfolds between Sandra and Albert in a darkened room.

"Sandra, during the last two weeks I've had the time to think deeply, probably deeper that at any time during the last 30 years. I know we have touched on some of these points at times; however, I greatly value my friendship with you over the past ten years. In some people's minds it could be described as love - but we both know the manifold threads of love are varied. People use the word, 'love' to describe a cake or pie, but in our case the word refers to a close sort of fellowship. But Sandra, as I travel into the past in my mind's eye, I am reminded of my first love, my late wife – Kim. I don't need to reminisce with rose tinted glasses because the intensity of feeling is just as strong as it ever was. I think these feelings, which humans are prone to, are designed to protect the species. If we are given time to detect and experience this depth of emotion then more families would be happy. It is always a sad sight when a couple are together only because of a kind of duty or responsibility to their children, or sympathy for a spouse - or even worse - when it's due to a fear of losing face or funds."

"Well said Albert! As you know I've been married three times. However, I now realize why the unions failed. When I met Ross and fell in love, only then did I realize what had been missing in my life. I will put it this way: do you remember the song that the rock band *Queen* sang? It was called, or it went *One day of love is worth more than a lifetime alone.*"

"No Sandra, I haven't heard that song but I can see the sentiment in the lyric. Sandra, I knew when you were in the depths of despair over Ross, I was in no doubt that your feelings for him were pure love in its God given quality. When I fell in love with Gwen, or should I say, when love found me to be honest, I had given up hope of finding love for a second time. I was in the process of making the most of my friendships. However, though

83

I am still alone with my feelings, I have warm feelings which I can call upon at any time. I am thankful for this gift."
"Albert, I am glad you to call you my friend."
"Thank you Sandra, if we get ourselves out of this predicament we will, I'm sure, have re-evaluated many aspects of our lives."
"Albert, I'm frightened, are you?"
"Yes I am Sandra, but we have to keep our chins up. Have I lost any more weight?"
"Albert, if you lose any more weight you will get a glimpse of your pecker for the first time in many years without the aid of a mirror!"
"Thank you Sandra, flatterer!"

Another change of scene; an image flickers into life on a TV screen. It is a grave, greying newscaster sitting in a studio.

"Good evening, this is Alvar Liddel reading the Nine O'clock News from the BBC. It has been reported today from our African correspondent – just a moment – we can hear now from Africa, our man Nelson Famela reporting from Cape Town."
"Thank you Alvar. Yes I have some information regarding the British couple who were taken captive by Somalian Pirates. I am sorry to say it is feared, this evening, that Sir Albert Longridge and his companion, Lady Sandra Brierfield have both been murdered. Apparently, the pirates had given a final ultimatum that if the ransom of seven million US dollars was not paid by noon today then the couple would be put to death."
"Nelson, are you able to confirm this information?"
"Yes Alvar, the bodies have just been released to the Somalian authorities and the British Consul in Cape Town have verified this. Now back to you in the studio."
"That was Nelson Famela reporting from Cape Town. Now, I am told that I can talk to Dame Janet Knowles, who is Lady Sandra Brierfield's sister, in our Manchester studio..."

There is a pause as the newscaster frowns, listening in concerned concentration. "I am sorry, Dame Janet is too upset to talk at the moment, but her husband, Sir Arthur Knowles, will answer my questions. Sir Arthur, can you confirm that Lady Sandra had given strict instructions that a ransom was not to be paid under any circumstances?"

"That is true. Also I would like to say that Sir Albert had made it quite clear to his eight sons that no ransom was to be paid as this would be the only way to curtail this abhorrent activity."

"Thank you, Sir Arthur. That was Sir Arthur Knowles in our Manchester studio. I can also report that the Prime Minister has paid his compliments to the bravery of Lady Sandra and Sir Albert. He said of Sir Albert that – 'the world would be a poorer place without him and his contribution to the literary world will be sorely missed.'"

Also in other news, the England cricket team will be without four star players for tomorrow's test match out of respect for their father. Sir Albert himself was a former captain of the MCC during a career spanning 20 years. Sir Albert's other sons are well known personalities in a number of fields. Daniel was a former captain of the London Irish rugby union team; while another – Thomas – captained the Welsh rugby union team. Benjamin - is an international footballer for Israel, and his youngest son – Sir Wilfred – is an internationally renowned interior designer. Unfortunately, they were unavailable for comments as they are all in Australia competing in the TV programme, 'I'm A Celebrity Get Me Out Of Here'. Lady Sandra's only granddaughter, the Right Honourable Lady Ava Gardener Brierfield was also unavailable for comment as she is on a film location in Los Angeles."

Summer Holiday

"It was just a dot on the horizon, hardly worth the eye strain needed to try to make out, so the men tried to rest underneath the canvas sheet. It was obviously very important to keep out of the sun's vicious rays. The night-time manoeuvres of the previous evening had exhausted most of the men. However, although for the next hour they kept glancing into the distance, the dot on the horizon was almost indiscernible. A few minutes later one of the men realized what it was:

'It's an Arab! But he's not walking normally, he's kind of crouched over and it looks as if he has something on his back.'

Meanwhile, the men had received their day's water ration, as usual the men complained but only to each other. It wasn't wise or healthy to allow your grumbling to filter through to your superiors.

'Not much is it? I mean, a pint a day, and in this heat,' said one.

'I know, I struck lucky yesterday, one of the wagon drivers from D Company made me a brew of tea from the truck radiator water, it was the best I've ever had,' said another.

Meanwhile, the Arab was now only about 200 yards from the camp.

'Blimey, he's taking his time; he's walking in a strange way.'

'Yeah, he's bent over with his hands on his knees. Talk about slow; he's in worse shape than us. Where can he be going?'

'It's certainly not here; he can only be heading for Tobruq.'

"Blimey! Where can he have come from? It can only have been Albardi."

'Hell, that's what? 15 miles at least and he's got another ten to go.'

Another 10 or 20 minutes went past.

'Look at that, I've never seen anything like it! It's almost unbelievable. I would not have believed it if I hadn't seen it with my own eyes, he's got a car engine on his back!'"

"Dad, is that really a true story?"
"Walter, that's as true as I'm standing here on the South Pier".
"Albert."
"Yes Mabel."
"What are we going to do?"
"Walter and me are staying up here on t'pier."
"Right! Me and Wilfred are going on t'sands."
"What, in this rain?"
"Yes! If we wait any longer it will be dinner time. We've already had four days traipsing from one shelter to another, so if you and Walter want to stay up here on t'pier it's up to you."
"Aye, we'll stay up here. We're going to watch the talent show, it starts at eleven. And Mabel..."
"What?"
"Make sure Wilfred keeps his pac-a-mac on."
"'Course I will, what do you think I am, a tuppence ha'penny?"
"Come on Walter, let's get a good seat."
"Dad, I don't know what we would have done without these shows. Are we going to the afternoon one as well?"
"Yes. I can't see the rain stopping any time soon. It's a pity for poor Wilfred, he's not had his mac off all week, but your Mum seems to enjoy sitting on the sands, even in the rain."

The next day, Albert arrives back at the room of the family's B&B. He carries under his right arm a newspaper and in his left hand a packet of cigarettes. He is perspiring freely. "Where have you been Albert?"
"Just been for a paper and some Woodbines. Mabel, it's cracking the flags!"

"About time! Would you believe it, and us going home tomorrow?"

"Ah well, we'll make the most of today, eh? What time is your mother and father arriving?"

"They should be with us at about 11 o'clock. Will you meet them off the train? Or they will never find us down on t'sands. It'll be heaving."

"Right Mabel. Get a spot on this side of the pier then I'll be able to find you."

"Right Albert."

"Wilfred, Nana and Grandad are coming today! Hey Mabel, look at his little face, it's lit up"

Wilfred pipes up. "Will Grandad give me a sixpence?"

"Mabel, did you hear that? He loves your dad, but only for his money!"

"Ha-ha!"

"Walter, will you keep an eye on him? Especially if he wants to go to the donkeys. He's only three you know; he's just a big lad."

"Right Dad, I won't let him out of my sight."

Albert arrives just as his in-laws walk out of the train station. He waves at them and goes over to say hello. "Morning Mother, morning Dad."

"Morning Albert, where's Mabel and the boys?"

"They're on the sands. It's a grand day Dad."

"Champion Albert!"

"Dad, you'll need your trilby today, it's cracking the flags."

"Wouldn't be without it Albert!"

Together they walk down the street outside the train station towards the promenade. Arriving at the promenade Albert wipes the sweat from his brown and licks his lips. He glances longingly at a cafe on the promenade. "Mother."

"Yes Albert."

"I'm just going to get a cup of tea for us. Wait here for me, there's a queue."

"Right-o."

After a while Albert returns clutching three cups of milky tea, sipping from one and trying not to spill the others.

"Right, let's see if we can find 'em. Don't think I've ever seen as many people down here before! Have you Dad?"

"Albert, just after the Great War, Mother and me were staying near t'Central Station and we were a bit late getting on t'sand. When we did there wasn't a deck chair left! There must have been at least 500,000 people on t'sands that day."

"Blimey!"

"Albert, don't take much notice of Dad, he's always spinning a yarn."

"Ok, Mother."

Albert and his in-laws arrive at the beach where Mabel and the boys have camped.   Mabel sees her parents and welcomes them one by one with a kiss.

"Morning Mabel."

"Morning Mother."

"Morning Dad."

"Morning pal."

The grandparents then move on to greet their grandchildren, Walter and Wilfred.

"Morning Walter."

"Morning Nana."

"Walter, where's your tie?"

"Mum said I could take it off, it's so warm."

"Well, keep you cap on, you don't want too much sun on your head, especially since you have ginger hair like your grandad."

"Ok Nana."

"Aah! Wilfred, come to Nana. Dad, let him go. Come here
Wilfred, what have you got? A sixpence! Where did you get that
from?"
"From Grandad."
"Will you save it?"
"No Nana, I want to go on a boat."
"Mabel, he says he wants to go on the boats."
"I'll take him." said Grandad.
"Are you sure Dad?"
"Yes, come on pal."

Wilfred and his grandad depart for the boats hand in hand.
"Mabel, do you want an ice cream?"
"Thanks Albert."
"Do you want one Mother?"
"No thanks. Don't get Dad and Wilfred one until they return."
"I don't need to ask you Walter, you're the ever open door."
"He's a growing lad. Albert!"
"Don't I know it, Mother. I don't know where he gets his height
from, our family are all short legged."
"He might get it from my brother, your uncle Harold in America.
He's quite tall, about five feet eight I think."

Mabel's father returns on his own, he appears to be in a highly
anxious state. "Dad, where's Wilfred?"
"I can't find him."
"Can't find him, what do you mean? Oh my god, Dad, you were
with him!"
"Yes, but they must have dropped him off further down the
beach!"
"You mean you didn't go on the boat with him?"
"No."
"You mean you just put him on it?"
"Yes!"

"Albert, you and Mother go along the water line. Me and Dad will walk down the centre of the beach."
"Right, Mabel."
"Walter, you wait here and watch this stuff, don't move away from here!"
"Ok Mum."
Both groups of adults move off leaving Walter to watch their belongings. He watches them move off in to the distance, praying silently for his brother's return. While the adults are away, Walter amuses himself by digging a sandcastle to distract himself. The waiting seems to go on a long time, however. Eventually, he spies his nana and dad returning in the distance.
"Dad, have you not found him?"
"No Walter, it's been half an hour now. I'm going up on to the prom! I'll report him to the lost children caravan."
"Very good, Albert" said Nana
Mabel's mother starts to cry. "Don't cry Nana, we'll find him."
"Alright, thanks Walter, you're a good boy."

Next, Mabel and her father arrive back at the camp. "Mabel! Dad! No luck?" asks Nana.
"No, it's like looking for a needle in a haystack."

Young Walter pipes up, "Mum, let me go, I can run in and out of these deckchairs. Let me go, I'll find him!"
"Alright Walter love, off you go. I'll go back down there; your Nana will stay here." Walter sprints off.

"Dad, will you go back to where you put him on the boat? Just in case he's made his way back to that point?"
"Right Mabel."
Mabel's father walks off back to the boats. When he gets there he sees a young boy sitting on the sands all screwed up with his head in his hands. It's Wilfred!

"Wilfred, Wilfred, there you are! Come here little pal! You're a brave lad and hardly any tears. Come on, let's get you back to Mum." Grandad and Wilfred walk hand in hand back to the camp. Some way off, Mabel spots them and runs over desperately. At the same time Walter returns and runs over joyfully to greet them.

"Wilfred! Oh thank God he's safe. Come here love!"

"Mum, he was sat on the sands all by himself; he was just starting to cry."

"Walter, go up on the prom and tell your dad we've found him."

"Right-o Mum."

Walter sprints off towards the prom and spies his dad near the railing, about to come back on to the beach.

"Dad, Dad! We've found him!"

Later on, Walter and his mum are talking about the day's events as she tucks him up in bed at their B&B. "Mum, it's been a strange day, hasn't it?"

"Yes it has Walter."

"Mum, why do you think Grandad put Wilfred onto the boat on his own?"

"Well, to be honest, I feel a bit guilty really. Because I should have said to Grandad, 'Make sure you go with him.' You see, Walter, Grandad was desensitized during the Great War, and so just a ride on a boat doesn't seem much to him. When I was a little girl my dad - your grandad - put me on a train in Burnley with a ticket to ride to Eastbourne, to stay with my Aunty Edith for the summer holidays. I was only eight years old!"

"That would be against the law now, wouldn't it Mum?"

"Yes dear, it would."

"Mum, when I went to tell Dad that I'd found Wilfred."

"Yes."

"Mum, Dad started to cry."

"Did he? Well you see Walter, your dad is the opposite of your grandad. You know it's only a few years since your dad came home from the last war. I know he tells you little amusing stories of when he was in the Middle East during the war, but when your dad returned from his last posting in the Far East, apart from the usual hardships felt during wars, your dad lost his best friend. They were patrolling an area that had recently been cleared of Japanese troops. His friend picked up a booby-trapped cigarette lighter and it blew up and killed him."

"Is that what makes him fuss a bit at times; you know, being a bit overprotective?"

"Yes Walter. Don't worry; he'll get stronger as the memories fade."

"Yes Mum."

"Night night, Love."

"Night night Mum."

Nana And Grandad

"Grandad, is it true you were the cleverest kid in the school?"

"Yes, it is true. When I was 12, the headmaster called me over and said to me - 'I can't teach you any more, you have completed the syllabus' - that means everything a child needs to know before they leave school and start their working life."

"What did you say?"

"I said, 'What am I to do, Mr. Hargreaves?'"

"What did he say Grandad?"

"He said I was to divide my time up in this way: during the morning, I was to report to the boiler room in the cellar under the school building and the caretaker would give me a shovel so I could stoke the boiler."

"Was that donkey work Grandad?"

"Yes it was, but there were some perks that came with the job because I took delivery of the milk. Every child was entitled to a small bottle of milk every day, however there was always two or three children absent, so I would drink two or three bottles. I didn't realize at the time, but later when I look back, I now know why I was so big and strong. Children don't get free milk nowadays. It was cancelled by Prime Minister Margaret Thatcher."

"Was that tight Grandad?"

"Yes, people called her: 'Thatcher the Milk Snatcher'."

"What were you to do in the afternoons?"

"In the afternoons I was to report to Mrs. Hargreaves – that's the headmaster's wife - and she would give me some chores to do: gardening, cleaning, shopping and other jobs which needed doing."

"Grandad, is it true you were the strongest man in the world?"

"Yes, that's true. As a young man I was walking home from t'mill, and was half way up Peel Brow, when I noticed a horse and cart. The driver was trying to get his horse to stand up. It had collapsed and was kneeling down and unable to get up. I walked over and got underneath the horse in a squat position. Then I stood up. The driver said that the carthorse weighed almost a ton weight."

"Blimey, you really must be the strongest man in the world."

"Dad, what are you saying to Shamus?"

"We're just having a man to man conversation."

"I know your conversations; don't fill his head with all that 'Walter Mitty' rubbish."

"Yes Mother."

Later that same day, Grandad is talking to Ada. "Grandad, why do some ladies look like men?"

"That's a strange question Ada, why do you ask that?"

"Well, when I went to the hairdressers with Mum there was a lady having her hair done and she had a moustache."

"Some ladies get facial hair when they are getting slightly older."

"Grandad, why are some ladies fat and ugly?"

"Don't say that pal, beauty is in the eye of the beholder."

"Well, it's just what I think."

"You see Ada, humans seem to blossom at different times in their lifespan. I find the range can be very wide. Sometimes a small child will blossom and, although the person grows up, they will never again show the same high quality. Whilst in others an academic or sporting success can bring a person to bloom. A woman in the middle or nearing the end of a pregnancy can look more alive than at any other time in her life. Whilst all humans are created equal it seems that some will never experience the joy a mother gets from holding a baby. When we consider the chance of any person being born at all, it's a sad sight when a

95

woman is unable to give birth, or a man never able to see his child suckle for the first time.

However, the emotions which God instilled in us all were put there for a reason. Long before we had a welfare state it was important for a woman and child to have protection and food et cetera or they wouldn't make it. To protect the species, God devised a cunning plan, a plan which can sometimes seem flawed in our current social world: when one sees the face of a man and a woman who are in love it's the nearest thing to an audience with the Holy Spirit. However, this is especially so when a woman falls in love, then, subsequently the man."

"Dad, what are you saying to our Ada? Don't be filling her head with a load of rubbish."

"I'm not Mother, we're just having a nice conversation. Get back to the ironing."

"What did you say Wilf?"

"Nothing Mother, I just said that I might do a bit of gardening."

Wilf moves off into the garden removing his pipe from his trouser pocket.

"Nana, why does Grandad talk so much?"

"The only thing I can think, apart from being old, is that he's an old gas bag."

"What's an 'old gas bag'?"

"It's just a saying for someone who talks a lot. Also, I think when your grandad worked in the mill it was so noisy, due to the machinery; none of the workers could speak because they wouldn't be heard. So they used to just move their mouths and in this way people knew what they were saying. It's called lip reading. So your grandad hardly spoke a word during the working week, and he worked in the mill for 55 years."

"That's a very long time Nana."

"Yes it is Ada."

In Search of the Light

I am sat looking at the daffodils in the shaded area of my garden. They are so tall; they stand straight up, searching for the light. It's the 18th of April 2018 and the warmest day of the year so far. By the way, my name is Rod Pilkington and I'm the writer of this true story. Due to my age some of my memories could be slightly askew, but the essence of the tale is as it happened.

"The sun is out, the sky is blue" - is the first line of a Buddy Holly song. Thinking of Buddy Holly my thoughts drift to the summer of 1958. I was 12 years old. I remember particularly two songs played many times on our radio. One was an Italian love song, *Volarie* and the other was called *Everyday* by Buddy Holly. The two songs could not have been more different.

At this time, I was obviously still attending school: a secondary modern. Back then, if you passed the 11+ exam you went to grammar school; but if you didn't you went my school. My school work wasn't anything to write home about. I enjoyed the practical subjects like woodwork, gardening, art and crafts etc. I also enjoyed writing essays some of which were read out to the class. Oh and sport, I enjoyed that. I played cricket in the school team. As for girls, I had not been attracted to anyone in my class. However, at times in the past I had had crushes on one or two, but they were usually much older than me. One girl was called Mavis Sandiford.

Mavis always had the lead role in our Sunday school pantos. I fell for her. I was seven and she was about 16. It wasn't a mutual admiration and there were several more unfounded mismatches. Anyway, there is a saying, 'Love is a magical thing'.

I think that's true but of course, we do hear stories of couples who meet and they don't fall in love at first sight, but in fact some time later. Some relationships just develop a bond due to having a familial, or a strong mutual caring feeling. They are all fine, but I don't think that they can be called 'magical'. Magical love occurs very rarely. It is unspoken and seemingly, without reason.

This is my story. I was at school. It was the midmorning break; many kids were milling about near the new lily pond which was set in the school gardens. I just happened to turn around and found that I was staring in to two brown eyes. I didn't know who they belonged to. Time stopped for me, and although we probably only held our gaze briefly, time seemed not at all to exist. As far as I know that was the first time that I had seen this girl. However, during the next few weeks we would somehow find ourselves automatically standing side by side at break times.

My feelings at the time were no more than a simple feeling of togetherness - but it was so lovely. At the end of the school day we would walk from the school gates to the railways station. I can't remember having any discussions or much conversation at all: after all what could a 12 and 13 year old have to talk about? It was enough just to be standing together. Her name was Jane Marney and something I must mention is that she had an identical twin sister called Anne. Anne had the same eyes as Jane and they both looked just the same, but Anne was just one of the many kids who went to our school.

When Jane left school to start her working life I didn't meet her again, only once seeing her sat on a bus heading for Ramsbottom as I was walking to Stubbins.

About 20 years or so ago, I was doing my day job as a painter and decorator working for a family at their home. The lady of the house had attended the same school as I had. She made me a cup of tea and as I drank it we chatted briefly. Then out of the blue and without any prompting she said, "Jane emigrated to Australia and has four children." I barely remarked on it at the time but later I thought: she has gone for the sun and warmth, in search of the light.

Epilogue

Most people are aware that the human race is at the dawn of civilisation and has quite a tenuous grip on survival. The scientists predict that it's only a matter of time when humans will be no longer around. Apparently, we are told that the life we have on earth is likely to be found on seventeen million planets the universe.

When we analyse man's intelligence we only have our own perspective to go on. Every few hundred years a brilliant mind appears, for example Newton, Einstein, Galileo. However, the human mind can't comprehend infinity, or the possibility of travelling faster than light. Nevertheless, some day in the future, I think we might be able to travel to other galaxies as I believe other life forms already have.

Don't expect strength from the weak, only expect strong
Weakness.
None are immune,
It could be you.

I dedicate this book to people who try, people who don't take 'no' for an answer.

Forever

How long is forever?
Will I ever know?
How far is infinite?
Will I ever go?
How did I land on Earth?
Where I started to grow
How high is Heaven?
Is that where they go?

Rod Pilkington 12th Feb, 2018

Printed in Great Britain
by Amazon